THE NEW JESSICA

"Where's the catch, Jess?" Lila asked.

"The catch," Jessica said, "is that we spend some time doing a little . . . well, a little transformation." She paused in front of one of the oval mirrors.

"Lila," she said triumphantly, her eyes still on her own face, "with a little ingenuity, I don't see why I ever have to be mistaken for Elizabeth again."

Lila looked worried. "As long as you don't plan on doing anything drastic," she said nervously.

Jessica raised her eyebrows. "Me? Drastic?" she said innocently.

But the secret smile she gave herself in the mirror said something entirely different. As far as Jessica was concerned, it was time for drastic action. She was sick and tired of looking exactly like Elizabeth. And she was going to insure that no one ever got the two of them mixed up again!

Bantam Books in the Sweet Valley High Series
Ask your bookseller for the books you have missed

SWEET VALLEY HIGH

THE NEW JESSICA

Written by
Kate William

Created by
FRANCINE PASCAL

BANTAM BOOKS
TORONTO · NEW YORK · LONDON · SYDNEY · AUCKLAND

RL 6, IL age 12 and up

THE NEW JESSICA
A Bantam Book / November 1986
7 printings through April 1988

Sweet Valley High is a trademark of Francine Pascal

Conceived by Francine Pascal

Produced by Cloverdale Press Inc.

Cover art by James Mathewuse

ISBN 0-553-27560-7

Published simultaneously in the United States and Canada

Bantam Books are published by Bantam Books, a division of Bantam Doubleday
Dell Publishing Group, Inc. Its trademark, consisting of the words "Bantam
Books" and the portrayal of a rooster, is Registered in U.S. Patent and Trademark
Office and in other countries. Marca Registrada. Bantam Books, 666 Fifth Avenue,
New York, New York 10103.

PRINTED IN THE UNITED STATES OF AMERICA

O   16   15   14   13   12   11   10   9   8

THE
NEW
JESSICA

One

Elizabeth Wakefield was curled up on her bed, oblivious of the California sunshine pouring through the open window into her bedroom. Elizabeth's blue-green eyes were thoughtful as she chewed on the end of her pen. She loved writing but found it required her most serious attention, especially writing in her diary—and most of all, writing about her new feelings for Jeffrey French!

But Elizabeth's reverie was shattered by the sound of running footsteps in the hall and urgent pounding on her door. Before she even had a chance to say a word, the door burst open, and her twin sister, Jessica, came flying into the room.

"Liz!" Jessica gasped, trying to catch her

breath. "Will you do me the biggest favor in the world and make dinner tonight? I promised Lila I'd drop over and see the clothes her father brought back for her from Paris."

Elizabeth snorted and snapped her composition book shut before her sister's curious eyes could see what she had written. "I'm really busy, Jess," she protested. "Besides, I made dinner almost every night last week. You know what Mom said. . . ." She let her voice trail off meaningfully. Alice Wakefield had her hands full, with two sixteen-year-old twin daughters and a career as an interior designer. She depended on the twins to help her prepare dinner each night, and the rule was, they were supposed to split the work equally.

Elizabeth sighed as she saw a desperate, pleading expression creep into Jessica's eyes. *Supposed to!* How many times had she heard that phrase where her twin was concerned? The problem was that Jessica lived by exceptions. It was always "just this once" or "this is a real emergency." Elizabeth, who loved her twin sister more than anything in the world, just couldn't hold out.

Elizabeth was the older twin by only four minutes, but sometimes she found herself slipping into the role of the older sister— protecting and indulging Jessica. For two girls whose looks were interchangeable, the Wakefield twins were almost total opposites. Elizabeth was the more conservative of the two. She loved reading, and her ambition was to be a writer one day, an ambition she fueled with long hours of work at *The Oracle*, the school newspaper at Sweet Valley High. Elizabeth worked slowly and steadily at her goals. She took her hobbies and her friendships very seriously. Not that she didn't have a great sense of humor or love to have fun—it was just that Elizabeth tended to think before she acted.

Jessica, on the other hand, was as quick-moving and hotheaded as her twin was responsible and sober. As far as Jessica was concerned, the most important thing in life was having a good time. She loved dances and parties, and she changed her mind about everything, from her favorite perfume to her latest boyfriend, with the kind of whirlwind speed that took her twin's breath away.

"Is there something wrong with your mirror?" Jessica was complaining now, frowning critically at herself in the full-length mirror on the back of her sister's door.

Elizabeth giggled. Jessica was attracted to mirrors like a magnet to iron! "I think it's probably OK," she said dryly.

"I look fat," Jessica moaned, sucking her breath in and pivoting before the mirror, her eyes narrowing as she regarded her slender waistline.

"You do not," Elizabeth said automatically, looking down longingly at her notebook. It looked as if her peace and quiet were ruined for good now. Jessica would probably convince her to make dinner, and the entry she had been writing would have to wait. . . .

Jessica scrutinized herself. She could see her twin reflected in the mirror, and it made her smile to see their identical images so close to each other in the glass. It was amazing how similar they looked. Five feet six and slim, they had identical sun-streaked blond hair, the same blue-green eyes, the same oval faces, and peaches-and-cream complexions. They even wore identical lavaliere necklaces, presents from their parents for the twins' sixteenth birthday. Jessica's eyes narrowed as they strayed from the mirror to the peach-colored knit dress hanging in her sister's closet. "Liz, can I borrow the dress Grandma Wakefield sent you?" she asked imploringly, her hand reaching out to stroke the soft fabric. "I'm so sick of all my clothes."

Sighing, Elizabeth pushed her journal away. "I don't know," she said, steeling herself. "I've only worn it twice."

Jessica took the dress out of the closet, held it up against her, and swirled in front of the mir-

4

ror. "It isn't fair. Why did Grandma have to send me that dumb history book when you got *this*?"

Elizabeth laughed. The twins' grandparents lived in Michigan, and while they didn't see their grandchildren that often, they frequently corresponded by phone and letter. "You were so enthusiastic about history the last time they visited, that's why," she reminded Jessica. Grandma Wakefield had gone back to school to study for a Ph.D. in the subject, and Jessica had found it totally—and apparently temporarily—compelling.

"Well, I'd much rather have the dress," Jessica repeated. "Come on, Liz. I just hate everything in my closet. *Please*."

"Oh, all right," Elizabeth relented. "But I refuse to make dinner tonight, Jess. You'll just have to tell Lila you'll see her later."

"You're the best twin in the whole world," Jessica shrieked. "I'm going to wear it tomorrow," she called over her shoulder, disappearing with the peach-colored prize in her arms.

Actually Jessica had never expected to convince her sister to make dinner; she was more than happy to put off seeing Lila until the next day. It was one of Jessica's tried and true tactics—make someone feel guilty about saying no about one thing when what she really wanted was the second thing she'd asked for!

Jessica hummed to herself as she hung the

dress in her closet. She knew she would look fabulous in it—a million times better than her best friend Lila, whose wealthy father bought her expensive clothing every time he took a business trip. Jessica and Lila competed with each other about *everything*. Jessica was glad she'd have something new the next day, too, just to make sure the competition was maintained at the highest level!

Elizabeth read over what she had written. It was funny how much writing in a diary helped to clarify her feelings, especially now, when she was experiencing the turmoil of falling in love. It had been so long since Elizabeth had gone through any of this, and it seemed especially exciting as well as especially risky. So much was at stake when you made yourself vulnerable to a boy who was still, in many ways, a stranger!

Elizabeth had had a long-term, steady relationship with a wonderful boy named Todd Wilkins. It might have gone on even longer if his father had not been transferred to Vermont. The move proved to be difficult for both of them. At first they had tried to maintain their relationship, agreeing that neither would date anyone else, but eventually they realized that this commitment was unrealistic. Elizabeth still valued Todd's friendship and enjoyed receiving letters from him, but their involvement was now a thing of the past to her. Since Todd, though, there hadn't been a boy who was special to Elizabeth. Until Jeffrey French.

Elizabeth felt her cheeks turn crimson as she recalled the embarrassing events of the previous weeks. Jeffrey was new to Sweet Valley. His father had sold the family tree farm in Oregon to accept a job in Southern California. Jeffrey was immediately accepted at Sweet Valley High. In fact within days everyone was trying to get to know him, especially the girls! Jeffrey's blond hair and outdoorsy, handsome looks really made him stand out. He was a star soccer player and a talented photographer with a strong interest in journalism. It was through *The Oracle* that Elizabeth became better acquainted with Jeffrey. The funny thing was that she was trying to get to know him, not because she was interested in him, but because her best friend, Enid Rollins, was! Elizabeth had promised to help Enid get together with Jeffrey, a task impeded by the fact that Lila Fowler had her heart set on him also. And naturally Jessica helped Lila.

At first Elizabeth hadn't wanted to admit how strong her own feelings for Jeffrey were. But eventually her emotions were no longer deniable: She had fallen in love with him. And Jeffrey clearly had eyes for no one but Elizabeth.

"It gets stronger every day," Elizabeth wrote.

"The funny thing is that I feel so much more alive—so much more myself. How can that be? Jeffrey is fascinating to be with. He knows so much, and he cares so much. The combination seems just right to me. Still, I find myself—I don't know—almost nervous, as if things are too good and they won't last this way."

Biting the end of her pen again, she stared out the window. What was it about falling in love that made her content to spend her time this way, just mulling over everything that had happened so far and looking forward to what was coming next?

"Liz!" Jessica hollered from the landing below. "Help. I think I did something really terrible to the soup!"

Elizabeth sighed and closed her journal. It looked as though Jessica was going to manage to get her way and force her to at least help cook dinner that night. When Jessica got embroiled in a kitchen crisis, Elizabeth thought, there was no telling what might happen!

"Well, how are my favorite carbon copies?" Ned Wakefield teased at the dinner table, looking from one twin to the other. Elizabeth grinned at her father. Dark-haired, broad-shouldered, and handsome, he was a more mature version of the twins' good-looking older brother, Steven, a student at the state university.

"Fine, Dad," Elizabeth said, helping herself to more broccoli.

Jessica glared. "Don't call us that, Daddy. You know I can't stand it."

Mr. Wakefield raised one eyebrow. "I've offended Twin Number Two," he said to his wife, who was bringing a basket of rolls to the table.

Alice Wakefield smiled warmly at him. Blond, blue-eyed, and slender, Mrs. Wakefield looked so young, people were sometimes shocked she had daughters old enough to be juniors in high school. "I'm sure Jessica is just kidding," she said lightly, setting the basket down on the table.

Jessica's eyes flashed. "I'm not 'just kidding.' Who wants to go through life as 'Twin Number Two'? Elizabeth and I are separate people with completely different personalities."

"What do you have to say to that, Liz?" Mr. Wakefield asked his other daughter with a smile.

Elizabeth grinned. "Ditto," she said, spreading some butter on a roll. Mr. and Mrs. Wakefield burst out laughing, but Jessica looked furious.

"This isn't a joke," she said angrily, her face turning red. "Liz, how can you act as if you don't care?"

"I guess I take it as a compliment when people

9

think we're exactly alike, Jess. Should my feelings be hurt that you seem to take it as an insult?"

"That isn't the point," Jessica fumed. "The point is—"

"The point is, you resent being teased about being a twin," Mr. Wakefield filled in for her. "Am I right?"

Jessica sniffed. "That's part of it," she said. "I just think it isn't very funny, that's all."

Elizabeth exchanged amused glances with her parents, and Jessica felt like kicking her under the table. She couldn't stand it when Elizabeth acted so condescending—as if she were a grown-up and Jessica were a two-year-old or something.

Jessica was sick and tired of being an identical twin. Jokes like her father's were starting to irritate her more and more. In fact, she was feeling so annoyed that she thought she might just have to do something about it.

The question was, what?

"I think you're lucky, Jess," Cara Walker protested as she regarded her friend. Jessica had sought refuge by convincing Cara and Lila to meet her for an emergency ice cream sundae at Casey's Place, a popular ice-cream parlor in the Valley Mall. "I always wished I had a sister,"

Cara added wistfully. "You take Liz for granted, Jess. Just think how much fun you two have being identical twins."

Jessica grimaced. "I must be forgetting how wonderful it is," she said, spooning a chunk of chocolate up from her Oreo sundae. "Listen, guys, I know exactly what's going on here. *Ingenue* magazine had a whole article on it last month."

"I thought they had an article on bad posture," Cara said and laughed.

Jessica gave her a dirty look. "The article was on identity crisis," she corrected her. "Don't you realize that's exactly what's happening to me? I'm *losing* myself! Do you realize," she added tragically, waving her spoon around for added emphasis, "that I don't have a single thing that belongs just to me? Think about it. Who does the Fiat belong to?"

"Supposedly both you guys," Lila said dryly, "but you seem to use it about ten times as much as Liz."

Jessica took another bite of ice cream. "Both of us," she said, injured. "That's exactly right, Lila. And what about doing stuff around the house? I bet you and your little brother used to do different chores," she accused Cara. "I bet he took out the trash and you did the dishes, right?" Cara's parents were divorced, and her younger brother lived with her father.

11

"Well," Cara said doubtfully, "I guess so. But—"

"You see!" Jessica shrieked. "You know what Liz and I do? We trade nights! She makes dinner one night, and I do it the next. We might as well be clones," she finished miserably, slumping down in the booth in despair.

"I must be dumb," Lila said, stirring her ice cream soda, "but I just don't seem to see what the crisis is, Jess. Don't you think you're making a big deal out of—"

"It *is* a big deal!" Jessica interrupted. "Don't you think an identity crisis is a big deal?"

"Why do you have to have an identity crisis?" Cara asked reasonably. "It always seemed to me that you and Liz managed to be pretty different in most respects." She and Lila exchanged knowing glances. "I wouldn't worry about people mistaking you guys, Jess. You're as different as night and day."

Jessica looked closely at her. "You really think so?" she said hopefully.

Cara laughed. "Come on, Jess! *Of course* you two are different! It would be really hard to confuse the two of you."

Jessica looked considerably cheered. "You're making me feel a lot better," she said, scraping the bottom of her sundae glass. "I mean, this article has really had me worried. The last thing I need is to feel like I only exist as part of a matched pair, you know what I mean?"

"I still think you're lucky," Lila said. "I'd give anything to have a sister."

Cara giggled. "Somehow I can't imagine it, Lila. You might have to share your wardrobe."

Lila gave her a haughty look. "She'd have her own wardrobe, of course," she said loftily. "I can just see it now," she added dreamily. "She'd probably be a year or two younger than I am, and she'd look up to me for everything. She'd probably follow me all over the place telling me how beautiful I am, how smart I am, how generous, how—"

Cara and Jessica burst out laughing. "That isn't exactly what it's like having a sister," Jessica told her. "For your information, it can be kind of a pain."

"I could understand this, coming from Liz," Lila retorted. "But what does Liz ever do to annoy *you*? She seems to be as patient as you can get."

"That's part of the problem." Jessica sighed. "She's so *good*. Can you imagine trying to compete with someone who spends most of her free time working on the school paper?"

Cara giggled. "But she likes it."

"I know—that's the whole point." Jessica was thoughtful for a minute. She was thinking back on the time, several months earlier, when she had become convinced her parents didn't love her as much as they loved Elizabeth. One thing had led to another, and before long Jessica really believed that she was the black sheep of the family. She had gotten involved with a guy named Nicky Shepard, who hadn't done much to help her stop feeling that way, and she had finally gotten so desperate she had actually tried to run away with him to San Francisco.

Jessica couldn't believe now she could ever have acted like such a dope. At least being the black sheep meant being different. It seemed to Jessica that her present situation was much more dangerous. She was beginning to feel that she and her sister really *were* carbon copies, as if there really weren't any differences between them that mattered very much.

It wasn't a feeling she could tolerate. And though Cara and Lila had cheered her a little, Jessica couldn't help feeling she had a major problem on her hands.

Two

Jessica angrily turned the combination dial on her locker, oblivious of the noisy stream of traffic on either side of her as her classmates hurried from their last-period classes. She couldn't believe what a horrible day it had been—and all because of Elizabeth's peach-colored dress! It was maddening. She had been expecting everyone to think she looked perfectly fantastic. Instead, the very worst thing in the entire world had happened. Even worse than being ignored.

Everyone had mistaken her for Elizabeth.

It had happened all day long. First Mr. Collins had practically knocked her over in the hall with a pile of papers he had for *The Oracle*. Under ordinary circumstances Jessica liked Mr. Collins, the strawberry-blond English teacher who worked as adviser for the school paper.

But not that day! Not when he had started rattling off about the paper and how urgent it was that she look at the proofs he had just received. Jessica had given him a frosty look. "I'm afraid you have the wrong Wakefield," she had informed him with just the slightest touch of asperity in her voice.

"Oh. Sorry, Jess," Mr. Collins said, his brow wrinkling in confusion. "I know what it is!" he exclaimed finally. "It's the dress. Wasn't Elizabeth wearing it last week?"

Jessica had turned crimson. She had forgotten that Elizabeth had worn the dress already. What an idiot she'd been to show up in something that everyone knew was her sister's!

The most humiliating moment by far, though, had come at lunchtime. As Jessica was maneuvering her way through the crowded cafeteria, she saw Jeffrey French hailing her from a table in the corner. Jessica felt heartened as she took her tray over to join him. She liked Jeffrey quite a bit, and though she was slightly disappointed that Lila had lost him, she was glad Elizabeth was the one who had stolen his heart. He really was cute and, to Jessica, a million times better than Elizabeth's former boyfriend, Todd, who Jessica had long tried to convince her sister was boring beyond belief.

No sooner had she sat down at Jeffrey's table than he had put his hand on her arm, very affectionately, and had started to discuss his plans for the weekend. Jessica had just stared for a minute before realizing that he had made a mistake. "Jeffrey, I'm *Jessica*," she had pointed out.

Jeffrey had jumped back as if he'd been stung. He turned bright red and kept muttering how sorry he was. And from the downcast expression on his face, it was apparent that he was disappointed as well. As far as Jessica was concerned, it was bad enough being mistaken for her twin sister. But realizing that people were *disappointed* to discover she wasn't Elizabeth was a million times worse!

Now, as she threw her books into her locker, Jessica couldn't help wishing she weren't a twin. Life would be much easier, she reflected, if she and Elizabeth were just sisters instead of clones! Sure, she and Elizabeth had always enjoyed the special closeness that came from their unusual relationship. But that day it seemed to Jessica that the dividends were too few and far between. She wanted her own identity. She was sick of being just one identical unit of a twosome!

Just then Jessica saw Lila hurrying past, a blank expression on her face. Lila had missed part of the day because she had had a doctor's appointment. Jessica wanted to remind her that they were going to the mall that afternoon.

Slamming her locker shut, Jessica chased after her. "Lila!" she called, annoyed.

Lila turned around, her eyebrows lifted. "Oh, hello, Liz," she said in the cool, slightly haughty voice she reserved for people she wasn't very close to.

Jessica felt herself begin to tremble with rage. "It isn't Liz, you idiot," she seethed. "It's *me*, Lila. Can't you even tell?"

Lila pushed a strand of long, light brown hair away from her face, her brown eyes narrowing as she inspected her friend. "What are you doing in that dress? Isn't it Elizabeth's?" she demanded.

Jessica felt her eyes fill with angry tears. "What difference does it make? Lila, I can't believe it! People can only tell Liz and me apart when we wear different clothes! It's like we're the same person!"

"You don't have to shout," Lila said calmly, regarding her friend with an expression of amused patience. "Jessica, dear, don't you realize that you and Elizabeth are identical twins? Why shouldn't people get you confused every once in a while?"

"Every once in a while," Jessica muttered as the two left the building and strolled out into the warm California sunshine. "How would you feel," she added suddenly, "if people thought

18

you were someone else? Wouldn't it bother you?"

"Who else could I possibly be? I don't even have a brother or sister, let alone a twin. There's only *one* Lila Fowler, Jessica."

Jessica glowered at the patronizing sound in Lila's voice. She wished Lila didn't sound so smug about it.

To be perfectly honest, she wished there were just one Jessica Wakefield right then. Or at least that there were something distinctive enough about Jessica Wakefield so people recognized her for herself!

"Now, tell me the honest-to-goodness truth," Lila said. She and Jessica were in the accessories department in Lytton and Brown, the big department store at the east end of the mall. "What do you think of me in this hat?"

Jessica thought that the pink straw hat made Lila look ridiculous, but she couldn't tell her friend what she felt. So she said, "I don't think so, Li. It just isn't you."

Lila frowned at her reflection. "Wait till you see some of the things Daddy brought me back from Paris," she said. "I'm not kidding, Jess. This time he's really outdone himself. These clothes are absolutely spectacular! I would have worn this wonderful leather skirt today, but"—

19

she regarded the clothes she was wearing—"I just bought this skirt and top last week and I wanted to wear it first."

Jessica didn't comment. It bothered her more than a little to hear the gloating tone in her friend's voice. Lila had always been given everything she wanted. Her parents were divorced, and that left Lila practically alone in the Fowler mansion—Lila and a staff of servants to take care of her. Mr. Fowler ran his own computer business, and he was out of town quite a bit. Jessica knew deep down that she much preferred her own family, but she would have happily traded the Wakefields' pretty, split-level ranch house for the Fowlers' sprawling mansion. And she wouldn't mind being a coddled only child right now!

"Hey, look at that," Lila said, pointing to the cosmetics counter. A sign saying Free Makeover had caught her eye.

Jessica sighed. Trust Lila, with her unlimited allowance, to be the first in line for whatever was being given away!

But when they reached the counter, Jessica's irritation evaporated. Transfixed, she watched the white-smocked cosmetics expert apply various gels and creams to the woman seated at the counter.

"You see, this will give your cheeks definition," the cosmetologist was saying. "Now I want you to go right upstairs and make an appointment to have your hair cut. Once I've finished with your face, you'll see how wrong this style is for your features."

Suddenly Jessica had an idea. "Lila," she said, grabbing her friend's arm.

Lila stared at her. "Uh-oh," she said. "You have that look on your face, Jess. That terrible I've-got-a-fantastic-idea kind of look. The kind of look that means big trouble!"

Jessica shook her head, her blond hair moving slightly. "No, this is perfect," she said. "Lila, I've just had a wonderful idea!"

"Don't tell me. Let me guess," Lila said mockingly. "You want to have a Lytton and Brown makeover, right?"

"Wrong!" Jessica said triumphantly.

Lila frowned. "Wrong?" she repeated, confused.

"Not a Lytton and Brown makeover. A Lila and Jessica makeover." Jessica giggled. She thought fast. "Lila, what are you doing this weekend?"

"Nothing special. Daddy's going to L.A., so I'll be alone. Why?"

"How would you like a guest for the weekend?" Jessica asked, her eyes twinkling.

"Jess, quit being so mysterious. What's going on?"

Jessica slipped her arm through Lila's and

grinned conspiratorially. "Nothing. I just thought I'd come over this weekend and keep you company, that's all. We can have a really good time, watch movies on the VCR, play records, have something really disgustingly sweet for dinner. . . ."

"And?" Lila said. "Then what? Where's the catch, Jess? It all sounds too innocent so far."

"The catch," Jessica said, obviously enjoying herself, "is that we can also spend some time doing a little—well, a little transformation." Pausing in front of one of the oval mirrors on the cosmetics counter, she fluffed her hair around her face and inspected her reflection.

"Lila," she said triumphantly, her eyes still on her own face, "with a little ingenuity, I don't see why I ever have to be mistaken for Liz again."

Lila looked worried. "As long as you don't plan on doing anything drastic," she said nervously.

Jessica raised her eyebrows. "Me? Drastic?" she said innocently.

But the secret smile she gave herself in the mirror said something entirely different. As far as Jessica was concerned, it was time for drastic action. She was sick and tired of looking exactly like Elizabeth. And it was high time she did something to insure that no one ever confused them again!

Three

"The thing about a makeover, Jess, is that you want to make really *subtle* changes," Lila said reproachfully, frowning with concentration as she applied a new shade of polish to her perfectly shaped nails. "Like this, for example," she added, extending one slim hand for her friend's inspection. "The very slightest hint of mauve—and my hands look completely different!"

Jessica narrowed her eyes at the cover of the *Vogue* magazine on her lap. "Subtlety is all right sometimes, Lila. But not this weekend. As far as I'm concerned, the only way we'll know we've succeeded is if my parents and Liz are ready to pass out when they see me tomorrow."

The two girls were sitting on the carpeted floor of Lila's enormous bedroom, fashion magazines spread all around them. It was ten-thirty Saturday morning. Jessica had spent the night at Lila's and wouldn't go back to her house until Sunday afternoon. No one suspected anything unusual was up. Mr. Fowler was often away on business, and Lila was always trying to convince Jessica to keep her company in the big house.

"See, I think something like this would be good," Jessica said suddenly, opening the magazine and pointing to a slim, sultry girl with sleek, black hair and striking, sophisticated makeup. "I need a whole new look—something kind of slinky and mysterious."

"If you want to look like her, you're going to need more than a makeover," Lila said, peering over Jessica's shoulder at the model's pouting expression. "You're going to need plastic surgery!"

"Very funny," Jessica said dryly. She dropped the magazine, scrambled to her feet, and crossed the room to Lila's enormous vanity table. "I think you're wrong," she added a second later, sucking her cheeks in and inspecting herself closely in the mirror. "With a little ingenuity . . . I'll need to dye my hair, of course," she added absently, lifting her blond curls off her shoulders.

"Dye your hair!" Lila shrieked, horrified. "Jess, your parents are going to *murder* you!"

Jessica grinned. "You didn't believe I was serious about this, did you?" she demanded. "Lila, let's get dressed. I want to go into town. We're going to need to raid the drugstore for some equipment!"

Lila looked upset. "Jess, I think you need to take it easy," she objected. "What color are you planning on dyeing it? What if it looks really weird?"

Jessica shrugged. "It won't look weird if we do it right. Come on, Lila. I want to look like that model in *Vogue*. Listen to what they say about her," she added, sitting down and grabbing the magazine again. " 'Katrina is the essence of the new European beauty . . . the daughter of a ballerina and a film director. Her hobbies include Indonesian cooking, French museums, and skiing in the Alps. . . .' That's going to be me, Li. No more kid stuff. No more of the old Jessica Wakefield." Her eyes shining, Jessica pored over the photograph of the seductive, sophisticated Katrina. "The makeover's just going to be the beginning! From now on, no one's going to mistake me for Elizabeth—not even for the old Jessica! It'll be as if a new girl had moved to town," she added breathlessly.

Lila looked wary. "I think you're going nutso, Jess. I just wish you didn't have to do it while I'm stuck with you for the whole weekend."

The smile faded from Jessica's face. "Don't be such a pain," she said, flinging the magazine down on the floor. "You're supposed to be supportive, Li. Can't you see I'm going through an identity crisis?"

Lila groaned. "Please," she said, blowing delicately on her left hand to dry the last coat of nail polish. "If I took every crisis you went through seriously, I'd be a nervous wreck. I think you're blowing this whole thing out of proportion."

Jessica thought fast. She could tell Lila was losing interest in the project, and she knew her work would be twice as hard without her friend's help. "Lila," she wheedled, "you know how much I need your advice. You're so good with makeup, and you know so much more than I do about fashion!"

Lila's eyes brightened. "That's true," she conceded. She thought for a minute as she examined her manicure. "You know, some of those clothes Daddy brought back from Paris look sort of like what Katrina has on in that picture. Maybe you could borrow some of them for a while," she said generously.

"Lila Fowler, you're the best friend in the entire world!" Jessica shrieked, throwing her arms around Lila so exuberantly she almost knocked herself off-balance. "Come on. Let's get dressed and go out for supplies," she added eagerly.

Jessica could hardly wait to get started. She felt

as if her whole life were starting over. She could hardly wait to create the new Jessica Wakefield!

Jessica and Lila spent hours that afternoon in the huge bathroom adjacent to Lila's bedroom. "I had no idea this was going to be so complicated," Jessica said ruefully, squeezing her eyes shut while Lila lathered her hair with the shampoo-in black hair color they had purchased at the drugstore.

"OK, now it says that this stuff will only last for two shampoos at the most. You'll have to keep applying it as long as you want dark hair," Lila told her, wrinkling her nose. "Ugh. It looks like finger paint." She giggled. "Like black finger paint!"

Jessica took a deep breath. "Well, who believes that stuff about blondes having more fun, anyway?" she said.

Lila laughed bitterly. "I don't know, Jess. Look what happened to me. Jeffrey French doesn't even seem to know I'm alive now that Elizabeth's snagged him."

Jessica sighed. "I feel really bad about that, Li," she admitted. "I guess Jeffrey just doesn't realize what a fantastic opportunity he passed up."

"Huh!" Lila said huffily, lathering away. "I'm

27

still furious with Liz. *I* think it's all *her* fault. If she hadn't started falling all over him—"

"She didn't exactly fall all over him," Jessica protested. Even though Jessica had been on Lila's side, she couldn't help defending her twin. She knew Elizabeth had been the last one to realize what everyone else had seen coming—that she had fallen in love with Jeffrey, and vice versa. "You and Jeffrey were wrong for each other anyway," she pointed out. "Wait until I make my debut as the new Jessica. You and I will really make waves! How much do you want to bet we both find new men?"

Lila grimaced as she tilted Jessica's head into the sink to rinse off the dark lather. "What am I supposed to be billed as—your hairdresser?" she grumbled. "Hey! This stuff really works!" she exclaimed a few minutes later, alarmed.

"Let me see," Jessica said, grabbing a towel. She spun around to face herself in the mirror, her eyes widening as her fingers flew to her damp hair. It was black. Raven black, just like the picture in *Vogue.* Jessica swallowed nervously. She'd had no idea what a difference it would make. Everything about her looked different. Her skin looked so much paler, her eyes so much more striking . . .

"Let's try styling it," Jessica said bravely, squelching her misgivings. She was going to look completely different, she reminded herself.

But however bizarre she looked, she wasn't going to be just one of the Wakefield twins. Never again!

"You know, it really doesn't look bad," Lila said thoughtfully, backing off with her comb in her hand. "Actually, it looks kind of—kind of exotic, Jess. I sort of like it!"

"You do?" Jessica said uncertainly. "But it's still wavy. I want to make it sleek, like Katrina's," she complained.

Lila squeezed some gel into her hands. "Hold still," she instructed. Jessica closed her eyes patiently, waiting for her friend to finish combing the cold, sticky stuff through her hair. "That ought to make it sleek," Lila said at last. "Now why don't you let me try the makeup tricks George showed me the last time I went to the Silver Door."

The Silver Door was the most exclusive beauty salon in town, and Jessica had always been jealous that Lila could afford to have her hair done there. George, the man who did her hair, had done makeup in Hollywood for years. "Go ahead," Jessica said. "But be sure to remember everything you do, so I can do it myself."

For the next half hour Lila labored while Jessica sat perfectly still, dying to look into the mirror to inspect her friend's work. "Now I'm lining your eyes with black kohl to bring out the blue," Lila would mutter, or, "Putting blusher up like this makes your cheekbones stand out."

Jessica began fidgeting.

"I want to see what it looks like!" she kept saying.

Finally Lila relented. *"Voilà!"* she cried, spinning Jessica around dramatically.

Jessica could hardly believe her eyes. Her hair hung straight to her shoulders. For the first time she could remember, her skin looked pale—delicately, exotically pale. Her eyes were the bluest she had ever seen them and were outlined dramatically with black pencil. Soft, dull-red lipstick completed the look. She looked foreign, slightly Eastern, and incredibly sophisticated. "Wow," Jessica breathed, turning her head slightly to examine herself from another angle. "Lila, I look so—so—"

"You look fantastic," Lila said admiringly. "And you sure don't look like a Wakefield!"

Jessica leaned forward and smiled. She sure didn't. The old Jessica Wakefield was gone for good!

"You're sure I can borrow all these things?" Jessica said doubtfully, looking at the clothes Lila had spread out on her bed.

"Sure. I've got dozens of things I haven't even taken the price tags off of yet," Lila said airily. She and Jessica had combed through the new clothes Mr. Fowler had brought back from Paris, choosing the most sophisticated ones. It was early Sunday afternoon, and Jessica was wearing one of the more casual outfits, a purple jump suit and lizard boots. She looked as if she had just stepped off the pages of a French fashion magazine.

Lila opened her huge, walk-in closet and took out a suitcase. "We'll pack everything in this," she said. "Otherwise, you'll never get it all home."

"Your family," Lila declared after they had carefully packed all the clothes, "is going to faint."

Jessica flipped her black hair back defiantly. "They'd just better get used to it," she said. She raised one eyebrow at her reflection, flipped her hair again, and tried a slightly different accent—a little more clipped. "I think I may drop by the bookstore in the mall on the way home and see if I can find some French novels," she said nonchalantly.

Lila stared at her. "What's wrong with your voice? Have you got a cold?"

"Of course not," Jessica said, more clipped this time. "Lila, darling, thank you so much for all your help. You've just been simply a *dear*."

"Darling?" Lila repeated blankly. "Jess—"

"I've got to *dash*," Jessica said quickly. By now she had it just right—a faintly British touch that went perfectly with her new European look. "I'll call you later," she added. And before the astonished Lila could say a word, Jessica had leaned forward to kiss her once on each cheek—an inspired touch, she thought. She had seen it in an Italian movie, and as she hurried down the steps with Lila's suitcase and her own canvas bag slung over one shoulder, she decided it was a habit the new Jessica would adopt.

Twenty minutes later Jessica had parked the red Fiat Spider she and Elizabeth shared in the Wakefields' driveway. She couldn't tell whether she was nervous or excited. But one thing was sure—her family would definitely notice it was Jessica this time. No one would ever mistake her for Elizabeth again!

"That must be Jess," Mrs. Wakefield said, looking up from the Sunday paper and listening to the front door opening. "Liz, run and tell her to be quiet so she won't wake Daddy, OK?"

Elizabeth nodded. She knew how much her father valued his Sunday-afternoon naps. In seconds she had crossed the living room into the foyer. But all thoughts of admonishing her twin fled when she saw the apparition that was coming through the front door.

"Jess?" she said fearfully, her fingers flying to her lips.

Jessica tossed her head and smiled. "Hi, Liz," she said, setting her bags down on the floor of the foyer. "What do you think?" she asked, twirling around. "Do you like the new me?"

Elizabeth felt the color drain from her face. She was so stunned, she could barely speak. "But, Jess," she choked out finally, "what have you *done* to yourself? What have you done to your hair?"

"Dyed it," Jessica said triumphantly.

"Girls," Mrs. Wakefield called from the living room in a stage whisper. "Liz, I thought I told you to tell Jess to be quiet!"

Elizabeth grabbed the table behind her for support. "You look completely different," she said accusingly. "Jessica, *why*?"

Jessica looked away from her twin's penetrating stare. "I just felt like a change, that's all," she said airily.

"Girls," Mrs. Wakefield repeated, coming into the foyer. Her mouth dropped open as she caught sight of her daughter.

"Hi, Mom," Jessica sang out.

"Jessica?" Mrs. Wakefield whispered, her eyes widening. "Jessica, what on earth—"

Elizabeth felt her lip begin to quiver. She wasn't exactly sure why, but she felt that Jessica had betrayed her. "You look like a stranger!" she cried, her eyes brimming with tears. Elizabeth couldn't bear to look at Jessica a second longer.

The hot tears spilling over, she turned and dashed upstairs. Elizabeth began crying in earnest behind the safety of her closed door. At times like this, only her journal helped her to sort out her thoughts, so she got it out and began writing.

"I can't believe Jessica would do a thing like this to me," she wrote furiously in her journal. "We've always looked exactly alike, and now she doesn't even look like my *sister*! I can't help thinking that she's done this because she doesn't want to be close to me anymore. And I just can't understand it."

Elizabeth reread what she had written. She wasn't certain why she felt as upset as she did by her sister's transformation, but it seemed to Elizabeth that something terrible had happened.

As if she'd lost her best friend, she thought sadly. Only worse. As if she had lost her twin sister, and nothing in the world would bring her back again.

Four

After dabbing a bit more lip gloss on, Jessica turned her head from side to side, inspecting herself in the mirror of the girls' room. It was Monday morning, and she was about to make her debut, about to walk out into the hallway and head for homeroom, letting her classmates see the new Jessica for the very first time. She smiled in anticipation. It was going to be quite a shock.

Now that she was beginning to get used to her new image, Jessica had to admit that she looked sensational. She had tied her dark hair back in a loose ponytail, and a few tendrils curled in wisps at her cheeks. Her eyes were darkened with lavish makeup—definitely sultrier than her usual look. White powder helped achieve the ethereal, pale effect she was striving for. And her outfit! Everything she had on belonged to Lila. Jessica was wearing an olive green leather skirt with a slit up the back. The skirt was so straight it was hard to walk. Matching hose with a lacy pattern and three-inch heels made Jessica's legs look longer and slimmer than usual. She felt very tall and elegant, and the silky, oversize blouse and green leather belt worn on her hips made her feel incredibly glamorous. Ordinarily Jessica didn't wear much jewelry—just her lavaliere necklace. Now, of course, the lavaliere had been removed. The new Jessica wouldn't be caught dead in something Elizabeth owned as well! According to *Vogue*, accessories made all the difference when it came to style. So Jessica was wearing a chunky necklace and big gold earrings. She smoothed her hair one last time and took a deep breath. The bell was ringing—it was time to try the new look out on Sweet Valley High!

Several minutes later Jessica pushed open the door to Ms. Dalton's homeroom class. The pretty young French teacher looked up in surprise as Jessica came in. "Can I help you?" she asked, obviously not recognizing Jessica.

"It's me, Ms. Dalton," Jessica said, enjoying the puzzled expression on her teacher's face immensely. "Jessica Wakefield."

Everyone turned around to stare, and a shocked intake of breath was audible.

"Jess!" Cara shrieked. "What have you *done*?"

Winston Egbert, the widely acknowledged clown of the junior class, jumped to his feet to execute a mock bow. "Ladies and gentlemen, behold—a transformation in our very midst!" he exclaimed.

Ms. Dalton was still staring at Jessica, her eyebrows furrowed. Within seconds the entire class was in an uproar. Girls were jumping up to surround Jessica, touching her hair, walking around her to inspect her outfit, exclaiming excitedly over the difference in her appearance.

"Sit down, everyone," Ms. Dalton said, looking annoyed.

But her words were ineffective. Jessica had created a sensation too great to squelch all at once. And clearly Jessica wasn't trying to squelch it—she was enjoying every minute!

"Where in the world did you get that outfit?" Caroline Pearce gasped admiringly.

"Oh, just some little place on the Left Bank," Jessica said, twirling her necklace and trying for the right expression—midway between total boredom and faint generosity.

"I think you look fantastic," Cara gushed. "I can't believe you had the guts," she added under her breath. "How did you—"

"I mean it," Ms. Dalton interrupted, her voice firm. Sensing that her irritation was genuine, the class quieted down. Students resumed their seats, but Jessica could tell everyone was still staring. And she loved it.

It was exactly the sensation she had hoped to create. And she knew with just a little effort she'd be able to keep them all swarming around her. Not just that day, either. The new Jessica was going to have them all floored for weeks to come!

When the homeroom bell rang, she was practically accosted. Everyone wanted to know where she had found the clothes, who had done her hair, what her parents had said, how long she was going to leave it that way, why she had done it, if Elizabeth had minded.

"Of course Elizabeth doesn't mind," Jessica said, changing her inflection slightly so she sounded slightly British again. She was walking down the hall, surrounded—Winston, Caroline, Regina Morrow, and Cara pumping her for information, and other classmates turning to stare. "Elizabeth and I are very different," she added imperiously. "Why should she object, just because I've chosen to be slightly more *daring* than I used to be?"

"I think you look fantastic with black hair," Caroline Pearce said. "You look stunning."

"I agree," Cara said loyally. "But aren't those heels a little high? You look like you're on stilts!"

Jessica looked at her best friend with disdain.

"Height," she said dramatically "is an important part of elegance, Cara."

"But now you're too elegant for me," Winston said mournfully. "I can't stand it. How will I ever convince you to marry me now?"

"Winston, *please*," Jessica said, wincing. "Now, if you'll all excuse me, I have to look at my magazine before my chemistry class." She removed a copy of *Paris Match* from her book bag as casually as possible. "It's so important to keep up with world events, don't you think?" she asked rhetorically.

Caroline gaped at the paper. "Where'd you get that?" she demanded. "I've never seen a magazine from France before."

Jessica glanced witheringly at her. "Really?" she said. She injected as much disbelief into those two syllables as possible. "Well, as I said, I think it's important to stay informed. There's a new play that opened that sounds absolutely marvelous. See you later."

With that, Jessica swept across the hallway, leaving the group staring after her in astonishment. She was actually having a hard time keeping a straight face. Jessica knew she had been a smashing success. Who cared what was happening in Paris? The best play in the world was taking place right here in Sweet Valley High, and naturally enough, she had the starring role.

Jessica had a feeling she had just earned herself a standing ovation!

"Is it my imagination," Enid Rollins asked, leaning forward with an inquisitive expression in her green eyes, "or have you been upset about something lately, Liz? You don't seem like your usual cheerful self."

Elizabeth sighed and pushed her tray away. Usually she loved nothing better than a good gossip session with her best friend, and the crowded cafeteria was the perfect place to observe her fellow classmates. But Enid was right. She wasn't acting normally that day. It had been a whole week since Jessica had changed her image, and Elizabeth was beginning to fear it was permanent. "It's Jessica," she said sorrowfully, her aqua eyes focusing on her sister, who had just entered the cafeteria surrounded by a crowd of admirers.

Enid glanced sympathetically in Jessica's direction. "Poor Liz," she commiserated. "It must be so weird seeing Jess looking like that!"

"Weird," Elizabeth said moodily, "is not the word. Enid, it's awful! I keep feeling like—I don't know, like I look for her and she just isn't *there*! It isn't as if she'd just gone and had a complete makeover, either. Because . . . well, I know this is going to sound dumb, but it isn't just *her*-

self she's changed. It's us. You know what I mean?"

"Sure," Enid said, patting her friend's arm reassuringly. Enid had been Elizabeth's best friend long enough to understand what she was going through. "You mean that Jessica's new look is kind of insulting to you, in a way. As if she doesn't want to be a twin anymore."

"She *doesn't* want to be a twin. That much is obvious!" Elizabeth's eyes filled with tears. "And it isn't just a new look," she added hastily, obviously fighting for control. "It's a whole new Jessica! She's wearing different clothes, reading different books and magazines. . . . She even sounds different!"

"I know," Enid said, wrinkling her nose as she licked some yogurt off her spoon. "I think she sounds really affected, Liz. Like Joan Collins on *Dynasty* or something."

"Well, I just wish she'd stop it," Elizabeth said heavily. There was a stormy expression on her face as she watched Jessica maneuver her way into the lunch line. Elizabeth had to admit Jessica looked terrific in the black silk jump suit and red high-heeled boots Lila had loaned her. Her sleek black hair was pulled back in a bun that day, with just a few loose wisps around her face. A red silk scarf completed the elegant look, along with oversize earrings that Elizabeth thought were just a little bit much for everyday.

41

"She sure is getting a lot of attention," Enid pointed out. "Maybe that's all she wanted, Liz."

"But Jessica *always* gets attention," Elizabeth protested. "I don't know, Enid. I think she's gone a bit too far this time."

"What do your parents think?" Enid asked curiously. "I don't think my mom would even let me go through the door wearing heels that high."

"My mom doesn't like it much," Elizabeth admitted. "But my father's convinced her to leave Jessica alone. He thinks she's entitled to do anything she wants to her appearance. You know my father—the great defender of freedom of choice!"

"They probably think she'll get sick of it pretty fast," Enid said thoughtfully.

Elizabeth shook her head. "I wish she would," she said miserably. "Enid, I can't tell you how upset I am about all of this! And the worst thing—"

She broke off in mid-sentence, seeing that Caroline Pearce and Olivia Davidson were coming over with their trays to join them. Elizabeth didn't want anyone but Enid to know how upset she was about Jessica. Enid and Jeffrey, that is.

She had been about to tell Enid that the very worst thing was that Jessica hadn't just been looking like a stranger, she'd been acting like one, too. She had practically stopped confiding in her sister. Jessica seemed to be spending every waking minute with Lila, and whenever Elizabeth tried to approach her, she went dashing off.

Elizabeth forced a smile for Caroline and Olivia, but her mind was a million miles away.

"Hey," Jeffrey called, panting a little as he hurried after Elizabeth through the crowded hallway.

Elizabeth turned around, the quizzical look on her face softening to the special smile she reserved for Jeffrey. It still caught her off guard, the way her stomach did little flip-flops when she saw him. It was all still so new and exciting! She couldn't help noticing, for instance, how nice Jeffrey looked. His blond hair looked so soft, and she loved the way his eyes crinkled up when he smiled.

"I saw you at lunch, but just when I was about to come over, you were accosted by a whole bunch of girls," he said, teasing. "Where are you heading right now?"

"The *Oracle* office," Elizabeth told him. "Mr. Collins asked me to check the proofs for the 'Eyes and Ears' column. Apparently the printer needs to have them earlier this week, so I said I'd pop in and look at them during lunch hour."

Jeffrey shook his head with mock disappointment. "Darn. I was hoping I could lure you off to somewhere wonderful." From the teasing expression in his voice, Elizabeth knew he was only joking. Since Jeffrey was working for the school paper as a photographer, she knew he understood how important it was to meet deadlines.

"Well," she said, dropping her eyes, "what about later on?"

Jeffrey's face lit up. "Maybe after school we could go for a drive. Remember, you told me you'd show me that wonderful canyon your parents used to take you and Jessica to when you were little?"

Elizabeth's eyes clouded over briefly, but with an effort she pushed the thought of her sister out of her mind. "I remember," she said, tucking her arm through his.

"Hey," Jeffrey said, "speaking of your sister, I can't believe what she's wearing today! And I just finished saying yesterday that I was sure she wouldn't be able to top that white gauze dress and those striped boots she wore last week."

Elizabeth's face darkened. She didn't want to think about Jessica right then—and she didn't want to talk about her either.

"But you know," Jeffrey went on thoughtfully, "I actually think she looks pretty good. I kind of like the idea of you two being so easy to tell apart."

Stiffening slightly, Elizabeth pulled her arm away. "Really?" she said flatly.

Jeffrey nodded, not noticing the dark look she shot him. "Really," he repeated. "I think Jess looks pretty good this way. In fact—"

Elizabeth bit her lip. "Jeffrey, I have to hurry. I promised Mr. Collins I'd have the proofs ready before next period," she said quickly. "I'll talk to you later, OK?" Without waiting for his reply, she hurried down the corridor, gripping her books tightly.

She couldn't believe Jeffrey could be so insensitive. Wasn't it obvious how upset she was about Jessica's behavior?

Maybe it was obvious, she thought miserably, opening the door to the *Oracle* office. Maybe it was perfectly obvious, but Jeffrey just didn't care.

From the sound of his voice, it seemed as if he was more than impressed with Jessica's makeover. Maybe, Elizabeth thought, Jeffrey had suddenly discovered he liked Jessica's new look a lot more than Elizabeth's old one.

Elizabeth felt like bursting into tears. She had been convinced that morning that things couldn't possibly get any worse. But now it seemed that the trouble was just beginning!

Elizabeth didn't even hear the door open ten

minutes later. She was sitting at her desk in the *Oracle* office, bent over the entry she had been writing in her journal.

I find myself going over and over old memories—all memories with Jessica and me in them. Like the times we wore identical clothing, trying to trick people. Or the times people came up to us in public places, like the mall, and made a big fuss over us because we were twins. In a way it always made me feel kind of glad when people thought I was Jessica. It reminded me that she and I share something other sisters don't.

I don't want to make too big a thing out of this, but I really feel lost every time I look at her and see this stranger staring back at me.

Jeffrey isn't making things easier, either. I guess I still feel pretty vulnerable and insecure about him. Sometimes I find myself wondering if he's really interested in me. Enid thinks I'm being totally nuts, which is typical of Enid. It would be so easy for her to feel uncomfortable about the idea of Jeffrey and me as a couple, especially when she had such a big crush on him herself. But Enid is the world's most generous friend. She seems to think Jeffrey and I are made for each other. She'd never believe it if I told her what just happened!

The way I see it, Jessica's new look is very glamorous. And no one could ever accuse *me* of being glamorous! Jeffrey obviously thinks she looks terrific this way. What can that mean about the way he thinks *I* look?

Elizabeth jumped when the door opened wider and Penny Ayala, the editor, came in. "Hi, Liz!" she said merrily, quickly walking to a worktable in the center of the office and beginning to stack up a pile of newspapers. "I have study hall next period, and Mr. Collins asked me to do a little housecleaning. I'm moving a bunch of stuff to the storeroom." She looked around the room. "This office needs cleaning out, that's for sure!"

Elizabeth hastily shut her notebook and put it under some papers on the desk. She loved writing in her journal, but she felt shy about letting other people know what she was doing—especially when she was supposed to be reading galleys. "Can I help?" she asked, getting quickly to her feet.

Penny shook her head. "I don't think so, Liz. I think I've got it under control. But thanks for offering anyway."

Elizabeth sat down and picked up the galley proofs for the "Eyes and Ears" column she had promised to proofread. Within seconds she had found an error, and several minutes later she was absorbed in her work. She barely noticed Penny walking back and forth behind her, lifting piles of things from one desk to the next.

That was what Elizabeth liked best about working on *The Oracle*—it took her mind off things. And that was exactly what she needed. In fact, she was so completely caught up in what she was doing that she didn't notice that Penny had picked up a pile of things on Elizabeth's desk and moved it over to the table.

Mr. Collins came in, just as Elizabeth had finished proofing the galleys. He looked at them quickly, then handed them to Penny, who was responsible for taking all the galleys to the printer. Just then, the bell rang.

"Well, Liz, I think that bell tolls for thee and me," Mr. Collins said cheerfully. Elizabeth was in his English class that period.

"I think so, too," Elizabeth agreed, getting up and walking out of the room with Mr. Collins. She had completely forgotten her journal.

It wasn't until she was halfway into English that Elizabeth realized she had left her diary lying on her desk in the *Oracle* office—right out in the open, where anyone who happened to come along could pick it up and start reading!

She was so frantic she could hardly concentrate on anything Mr. Collins was saying. All she could think about was her journal. What if

Jeffrey happened to go into the office and see it there?

Elizabeth could never remember an hour going by as slowly as that one did. It seemed as if each minute went more slowly than the one before it. Finally, the bell rang. Elizabeth almost bumped into John Pfeifer, sports editor of *The Oracle*, in her haste to get to the door.

"Whoa! Where's the fire?" he called after her good-naturedly.

Elizabeth didn't stop to respond. Once out the door she raced down the corridor, her heart thudding. She couldn't believe she had been so stupid! Her mouth dry, she wrenched open the door to the *Oracle* office, raced to her desk, and stared down at it in disbelief.

Her very worst fears were confirmed. The journal had disappeared.

Five

Jessica flicked a lock of sleek black hair from her eyes, aware that everyone was watching as she strolled down the corridor. Her aloof, slightly nonchalant expression belied the pleasure Jessica felt at each and every glance. She couldn't believe how much fun it was to come to school now! Everywhere she went, she created a stir. In the ladies' room she was always accosted with curious questions about what she was using on her hair, about her fabulous new makeup and incredible new clothes. Jessica edited her comments, as she saw no reason why she should credit Lila with her high-fashion outfits. "You know how it is," she told Olivia Davidson as they stood together at the mirror. "No matter how good a look is, it gets stale after a while.

51

Every woman needs to change her style from time to time." Jessica began outlining her eyes with a black kohl pencil.

"You're so lucky, Jess," Caroline Pearce said enviously, running her fingers through her red hair. "I don't even think a new look would make me look like you do."

Eyebrows lifted, Jessica inspected the redhead. Secretly she couldn't agree more, but she didn't dare tell poor Caroline as much. The girl wasn't that bad, anyway, especially now that she was so obviously one of the new Jessica's biggest fans. "Still," Jessica said ambiguously, "change is *the* word in fashion, Caroline." Jessica returned the kohl pencil to her bag, looked at herself once more in the mirror, then left the ladies' room and headed down the hall to the cafeteria.

What Jessica didn't add was that *change* was affecting more than just the exterior Jessica Wakefield. Since her startling transformation, Jessica felt—and was behaving—like a completely new person. Though neither she nor Elizabeth had ever had to diet to maintain their slender figures, Jessica suddenly decided it was time to lose weight. The fashion models in *Vogue* were gaunt, and Jessica had pledged to live on yogurt and carrots until she had lost at least five pounds. "All you do anymore is suck your cheeks in and stare at yourself in the mirror,"

Elizabeth had complained the night before, staring balefully at her twin. Jessica had ignored her. Elizabeth didn't understand *anything*, Jessica thought. Elizabeth acted as if she, Jessica, had committed treason, just because she wanted a little individuality. Elizabeth kept moping all over the place, giving Jessica pained looks whenever she saw her.

Luckily, that wasn't often. Before Jessica's makeover she and Elizabeth were often together. But Jessica's new independent phase had changed all that. She was making a conscious effort to spend more time away from home, even going as far to drive to the library at night to study or—admittedly more often—to meet Lila at L'Autre Chose, the chic little coffee bar Jessica had discovered a few blocks from the mall.

The trouble was that even Lila was starting to complain about Jessica's new image. "You're getting really weird," Lila had said the night before when Jessica ordered an espresso coffee and pulled a foreign magazine out of her bag. "What's the matter with you? Robin Wilson told me you missed cheerleading practice twice."

"Cheerleading," Jessica had retorted, wrinkling her nose, "is so childish, Lila. I'm thinking of starting ballet lessons again instead. Ballet is so artistic and elegant, don't you think?" Jessica had taken ballet lessons when she was younger but had dropped them when she got too busy to continue. Lately cheerleading had taken up so much time, she could never have considered dance lessons. But cheerleading really seemed to be part of the old Jessica's image—not sleek and sophisticated at all.

"I think you'd better cut it out," Lila had said darkly, glaring at the tiny cup of strong coffee the waitress brought her friend. "That stuff looks like sludge," she commented.

Jessica took a tiny sip, trying not to let her face show how awful it tasted. "Delicious," she had said with effort, sitting back in her chair and trying for the slightly faraway, exotic expression that cover girls seemed to come by naturally.

"Jess, what's wrong with you? It looks like your eyes are hurting you!"

Jessica had sat straighter, annoyed. "The trouble with you, Lila, is that you just don't understand elegance," she had snapped.

Jessica felt that everything that had been part of her old identity ought to be completely buried. Cheerleading, sorority meetings, school dances, long afternoons at the beach—all of those things seemed incredibly childish now. For one thing, Jessica didn't want to be in the sun very much now that she was trying so hard to cultivate a pale, ethereal look. The sun was bad for one's skin, anyway. And cheerleading just seemed ridiculous. Wearing those costumes was so tacky! Jessica was spending as much time as possible developing her new, sophisticated image. She had even gone to see a foreign film the other evening and had raved about it later to Lila, never admitting that she hadn't been able to read half the subtitles because she was sitting so far back.

Now, reaching the cafeteria, Jessica threw back her shoulders and took a deep breath. She loved nothing better than making an entrance, and she knew all eyes would be on her that day. She was wearing an outfit she had found just the other day at Lisette's—and had even risked putting it on her mother's charge, it was so fabulous. It was a white, really slim-cut skirt that was several inches longer than what she usually wore, with a white sweater with sequins on it. A white beret completed the look. With her new dark hair, the combination was fantastic. Jessica swept into the cafeteria, enjoying the intake of breath as she strolled over to join Lila at a far table.

"Jess, you look fantastic!" DeeDee Gordon exclaimed, hurrying over to join them.

Lila grimaced and picked at her spaghetti and meatballs. Lila obviously would have preferred it if DeeDee had kept her distance, but Jessica, enjoying the flattery, smiled winningly at her. "Thanks," she said, smoothing her new cotton skirt down over her legs. "I just picked this little thing up at Lisette's. Isn't it sweet?"

"Why aren't you eating, Jess?" Lila demanded suspiciously. "Aren't you feeling well?"

Jessica adjusted her beret self-consciously. "I'm watching my figure, actually," she said, eyeing the big forkful of spaghetti Lila was just lifting to her mouth. She was thinking that *actually* was a word she would have to use more often. It sounded so British. "Actually," she said, trying it out again, "I'd like to lose another three pounds. You can never be too thin."

"Or too rich," Lila said with a smirk, taking another bite of spaghetti.

DeeDee stared at Jessica, her brown eyes rapt. "I think you look out of this world," she said finally. "Jess, you should think about modeling. You look like you belong on the cover of a fashion magazine right now!"

Jessica considered this for a minute, trying not to watch Lila eat. Her stomach was rumbling a little, and she suddenly had an overwhelming desire for a good old American hamburger. "Thank you, DeeDee," she said. "Do you really think so?"

"I do. I really do," DeeDee gushed. "I'm not kidding, Jess. You should look into it. Remember when Regina Morrow was on the cover of *Ingenue* magazine? Well, now that you have dark hair and everything, you look just like that type. You're every bit as pretty as Regina," she added loyally.

Jessica's eyes narrowed as she looked thoughtfully at DeeDee. As a matter of fact, maybe it wasn't such a bad idea. Regina had certainly garnered a lot of attention when Lane Townsend had discovered her and had selected her to be on the cover of *Ingenue*! People had talked about little else for ages. True, Regina was a special case. Not only was she incredibly beautiful, but also she had overcome a serious handicap. She had been born deaf, but through years of special training and hard work had learned to live a normal life. And now, after a series of special treatments in Switzerland, Regina was back in Sweet Valley, her hearing almost entirely restored.

"Regina's different," Lila interjected, looking irritated. Lila had been very jealous of Regina's success at Sweet Valley High and had tried her hardest to beat her out of the *Ingenue* cover contest. She had wangled an appointment with Lane Townsend, but to no avail. He had told her she would never photograph well. Lila scowled, recalling how humiliating the whole thing had been.

Jessica smiled sunnily at her. "I think DeeDee's idea is a great one," she said, knowing what a sore subject modeling was with Lila and enjoying her friend's discomfort. "I think I just may have to look into it! Thanks, DeeDee," she added generously, turning away from Lila's scowl.

In fact, Jessica was completely mesmerized by the idea. "It really does make sense," she added thoughtfully. "I wonder if—"

"I know the name of a really good fashion photographer if you want it," DeeDee chirped, obviously eager to continue with the subject. "You know my dad's a talent scout, and a lot of times he needs photos of actors. Look, here's his card. Do you want it?" she added, rummaging in her bag and producing a slightly worn business card.

"Simon Avery," Jessica read from the card. "Sure, DeeDee. And thanks a lot!"

Jessica didn't know how seriously to take the idea, but she was intrigued all the same. And she had a hunch she could do far worse than to give Simon Avery a call and make an appointment to meet him.

Fighting for self-control, Elizabeth took a deep breath. "And you're sure no one's turned it in today?" she asked Mr. Collins, her voice shaking.

Mr. Collins looked at her with concern. "I feel terrible about this, Liz. You say it's a black-and-white composition notebook, right?"

Elizabeth nodded, her eyes filling with tears. "I left it in the office yesterday," she whispered.

"And when I came back after English, it was gone. I thought—"

"Now, let's use our heads," Mr. Collins said thoughtfully. "There really isn't any place it can have disappeared to, Liz. It has to be around somewhere!"

"Unless someone took it," Elizabeth said miserably.

"Now, who would do something like that?" Mr. Collins demanded. "Cheer up, Liz. I'm sure we'll get to the bottom of this before long."

But Elizabeth couldn't be consoled. She had been a nervous wreck ever since she had realized the journal was missing. What an idiot she'd been, just leaving it lying around. She had confided some of her most private thoughts in that journal. She could feel her cheeks burn as she recalled some of the more intimate things she had written.

She couldn't bear the thought of anyone finding her journal. But the more she thought about it, the more likely it seemed that that was exactly what had happened. Someone had obviously come into the office, seen the notebook, and scooped it up. And the whole time she'd been sitting in Mr. Collins's class in complete agony, realizing she had left it just lying on the desk!

"Listen, why don't we put a card on the bulletin board?" Mr. Collins said, patting her hand sympathetically. "I promise, Liz, someone will turn it in. There's obviously been a mistake of some sort."

"All right," Elizabeth said listlessly, trying to muster up a smile of appreciation. She knew Mr. Collins was doing everything he could think of. If only—

Her thoughts were interrupted as the door to the office swung open and Jeffrey came in, camera in hand. "Hey," he said, breaking into a big smile.

Elizabeth shot Mr. Collins a quick look. She didn't want Jeffrey to find out the journal was missing, though she wasn't exactly sure why. Mr. Collins gave her a reassuring wink. "I'll see you two later," he said, pressing Elizabeth's hand as if to signal they would resume their conversation later on—alone.

"I've been looking everywhere for you," Jeffrey said softly when Mr. Collins had left them alone in the office.

Elizabeth cleared her throat nervously. "Really? I was right here all along," she said. She wished she could make her voice sound as playful as his. Even better, she wished she *felt* playful. Losing that journal just had her tied up in knots. She was as tense as she'd ever been and she felt that if she heard one wrong word, she would burst into tears.

"You look pretty terrific," Jeffrey said huskily, putting his hands on her shoulders and staring deeply into her eyes. "You know, I kind of like it now that you Wakefield twins are so easily identifiable."

"What do you mean?" Elizabeth asked.

Jeffrey smiled and shrugged. "You know, it's just nice, knowing that you're not sharing your looks with Jessica anymore."

"You think she looks terrific, don't you?" Elizabeth demanded.

Jeffrey tilted his head to one side, considering. "She looks *different*. That's what I like."

"Oh, I see," Elizabeth said, pulling away. She felt annoyed by Jeffrey's attitude about Jessica. If he thought Jessica looked so fantastic now, why didn't he just come right out and admit that he'd rather spend time with her than with Elizabeth?

She was sure that was what was going on behind his casual comments. Elizabeth felt vulnerable when it came to Jeffrey French, and she felt most vulnerable when the subject of Jessica's new appearance was broached.

The thing was, she and Jeffrey were still just in the beginning phases of their relationship. She cared about him a lot. But she felt as though she still didn't know him that well. It was hard to judge exactly what he was thinking and feeling.

She felt more than a little insecure. And right then she felt more strongly than ever that she had followed her heart too quickly.

Jeffrey really didn't care for her at all, she

decided suddenly. He was much more interested in Jessica. And if that was the way he felt, she'd rather find out right now, before she was even more deeply involved with him!

Close to tears, Elizabeth made some excuse to leave the office without Jeffrey. She suddenly felt she had to be alone. She had to sort out her feelings and decide what the best move was right then.

And above everything else, she had to find her journal. She knew she wasn't going to have a moment's peace and quiet until she was holding it again in her hands!

Six

It was Thursday afternoon, and Jessica was sitting in the waiting room of the plant-filled offices of Avery and Dennis, Photographers, waiting for her appointment with Simon Avery. She kept glancing appreciatively around her. The furniture in the waiting room was sleek and contemporary, and the walls were covered with photographs of glamorous women and handsome men.

Jessica cleared her throat nervously. "Do you think Mr. Avery will be much longer?" she asked the receptionist. She was late for cheerleading practice already, and while she had made up her mind that it was just kid stuff anyway, she didn't want to lose her coveted position as co-captain. Not yet, anyway. Not before she was well launched in her new career as a successful model.

"It shouldn't be much longer," the receptionist promised her, smiling.

Jessica crossed her legs, admiring the silky new stockings she had found. They were just the right shade of blue to match the two-piece knit dress she had convinced Lila to lend her. Jessica leaned back on the couch, imagining Simon Avery's excitement when his new cover girl walked into his office. She could hardly wait. Within weeks she would be catapulted into fame and fortune: People would be stopping her on the street for autographs all the time; guys would be fighting just for the chance to walk next to her in the hall. But Jessica knew she would be a good sport about it. Just like Brooke Shields. She could imagine what she would tell interviewers when they asked her how she managed to maintain such a natural life, despite her meteoric rise to fame. "Oh, it's nothing," she would say modestly, tossing back her silky black hair. "I really was modeling as just kind of an extra thing—a hobby, really. What I'm really interested in is acting."

Jessica closed her eyes, imagining the house in Beverly Hills she would buy once the money started pouring in. She would throw huge parties for all her famous friends; and people would come and have a blast and casually ask who the hostess was, then practically faint when they realized it was just sixteen-year-old Jessica Wakefield. She might have to change her name, Jessica thought suddenly. Jessica Wakefield sounded too wholesome. Maybe Jessa would be better. Jessa Fields.

"Miss Wakefield?" a pleasant voice was inquiring.

Jessica's eyes flew open. "Uh—yes, I'm Jessica," she mumbled, jumping to her feet.

"I'm Simon Avery," the man told her. He looked at her intently. "Why don't you come to my office, and we can talk."

Jessica was trying hard to regain her composure. "What a lovely office you have," she said, getting the faintly British intonation back into her voice.

"Thank you," Mr. Avery said, opening a glass door and offering Jessica a plush chair in his spacious office. "Are you from this area?" he asked, taking a seat behind his desk. He was a pleasant-looking man in his thirties, more professional looking than Jessica would have expected a photographer to be. With his horn-rimmed glasses, he looked more like a lawyer or a businessman.

"Yes, I've lived in Sweet Valley all my life," Jessica admitted, wishing she could claim she'd been born in Paris.

"Really? You have a slight accent," Mr. Avery said, looking closely at her.

Jessica raised her eyebrows, meeting his gaze unflinchingly. "Do I really?" she said at last. Her composure regained, she was beginning to enjoy herself. "Mr. Avery, I'd like to have some photographs taken. I'm thinking of trying to break into modeling," she explained. "Do you do that sort of thing?"

Mr. Avery chuckled. "Yes, of course I do." He looked at her again, frowning a little. "Yes . . . I think you just might do," he added, half to himself.

Jessica's heart began to beat a little faster. This was it. He was recognizing her as his new cover girl, just the way she had dreamed! "Do for what?" she demanded eagerly.

"Jessica, I've expanded my business quite a bit in the last year or two, and I'm now an agent as well as a photographer. That is to say, when people are looking for a certain kind of model they often let me know, since girls come here all the time to have composites made. Usually these jobs call for runway models at local stores. Sometimes I get requests for models for catalogues as well. It just so happens that Mr. Mahler, the art director at Lytton and Brown, just called me. That's why I was a few minutes late. And he's looking for a young woman to model some new fashions at the store two weeks from Saturday. I'm sure you're aware that for most modeling, you're too short. But Mr. Mahler is looking for models for junior clothes, and junior models tend to be shorter."

Jessica hadn't thought about her height being against her. She was sure there would be plenty of big-city agents at the Lytton and Brown show who wouldn't care about her height. The show would be a great place to be discovered. "What do I do to apply for it?" she asked.

Mr. Avery smiled. "Well, the first thing to do is to have some pictures taken. I won't have time to do it myself, but I can arrange to have my assistant photograph you." He looked her over critically. "You'll need about six or seven shots—a full front photo, a close-up, a profile, a few others. Then we'll put together a folder for you with a brief bio, your name, address and phone number, your height, weight, dress size, and measurements. Mr. Mahler is supposed to come in next Monday to go over the folders and make his final choice. If we hurry we should have your pictures ready by then."

Jessica was beginning to get excited. "And you really think I might be right for the job?"

"Well, I never like to make promises," he told her, smiling. "And Mahler may have a different sort of look in mind. But you seem perfect to me. You have a really distinctive, sophisticated look—slightly European, very cool and polished. I think Mahler will like that."

Jessica's eyes shone. "Does the job pay a lot?"

she asked, suddenly remembering the charges she had made at Lisette's.

"Well, it's five hundred dollars for six hours of work. That sounds pretty good to me for your first modeling job," Mr. Avery told her. "Of course, we take a ten-percent agents' fee. And the photographs will cost you a hundred twenty-five dollars."

Jessica jumped to her feet, her eyes bright. Five hundred dollars! She was already imagining the fantastic new clothes she'd be able to buy.

"I'll have to borrow some money from my parents," she told him. "Can I make an appointment to have the pictures taken right away?"

"Sure. Why don't you talk it over with your parents and call us back late this afternoon or early tomorrow morning? We'll be able to fit you in about this time, if that's good for you. If your parents say it's all right, I'll give you all the details on what clothes to bring when you call."

Jessica felt as though she were floating as she thanked him and said goodbye. She couldn't believe her luck. She knew some girls had to wait ages before breaking into modeling. And here she was, practically guaranteed a runway job at Lytton and Brown in just two weeks!

She couldn't wait to get home and tell her parents. Even cheerleading practice was going to be fun now that she could let everyone know about her sudden jump into the glamorous world of modeling and high fashion!

"I can't stand it," Elizabeth said miserably. She was in the backyard with Enid, dangling her long legs in the Wakefields' swimming pool. But she was too distraught to appreciate the warmth of the late-afternoon sunshine. "Enid, I confided everything in that journal! If someone has it—"

"You can't think that way," Enid said, sliding into the pool and gasping a little as the cold water came up around her waist. "Look, there's probably some prefectly reasonable explanation. Are you absolutely positive you left it in the *Oracle* office?"

Elizabeth stared glumly down into the water. "I'm positive," she said mournfully. "Enid, I'm done for if anyone finds that notebook. That's all there is to it."

"You know what I think?" Enid asked, as she dogpaddled in the water. "I think the diary isn't the only thing bugging you. Are you sure you're all right?"

Elizabeth bit her lip. There was nothing she wanted more than to confide in Enid right then. She just wasn't sure she could explain what she was feeling.

"Is everything OK with Jeffrey?" Enid probed

gently, coming over to the side of the pool where Elizabeth was sitting.

Elizabeth's eyes filled with tears. "Not really," she admitted. "Oh, Enid, I feel like such a jerk! I've just rushed into the whole thing. I feel like I've made a fool out of myself."

"Why?" Enid asked, confused. "Is something the matter?"

"I don't think—well, I just don't think Jeffrey really feels the same way I do. I keep feeling as if—"

"Spit it out," Enid said. She laughed sympathetically. "You're not making any sense, Liz."

"Well, he keeps gushing over the way Jessica looks," Elizabeth said miserably, kicking one foot in the water. "It makes me feel terrible, Enid. I mean, I never even had to consider being jealous of Jessica before. It makes me feel terrible to even admit it, but I'm afraid Jeffrey likes her better than me."

Enid stared at her, astonished. "Has he given you any reason to think that?"

Elizabeth bit her lip unhappily. "He talks about her new look all the time. He's always saying how great she looks with dark hair, and complimenting her clothing. I just keep getting this feeling that he's trying to give me a message."

Enid's green eyes filled with compassion. "Have you tried talking to him about it?"

"Well, that's just the thing. I know I should,

but I feel like—well, I feel like Jeffrey and I haven't really had a big serious talk yet. We're so new together! And I feel too scared to bring it up."

"Well, you know what you'd say to me in similar circumstances," Enid pointed out. "You would say that it's a lot better to bring it up than just to let things smolder. Sooner or later he's bound to notice how upset you are."

"Yes," Elizabeth said faintly, staring down at the water. "I guess you're right. . . ."

But she couldn't really imagine approaching Jeffrey about it. It just seemed too mortifying to admit she was jealous of her own twin!

"I can't believe it," Jessica cried, her eyes flashing. "My very own parents aren't even excited about the biggest break in my whole life!"

"All we said is that we think you should be cautious, Jess," Mr. Wakefield said mildly, helping himself to salad. "You're sure that this Mr. Avery can get you the job at the department store?"

"What your father is trying to say, in his usual gentle fashion, is that you're going to be heavily in debt to us if the job doesn't come through," Mrs. Wakefield pointed out, coming over to the table with a frown. "A hundred twenty-five dollars is a lot of money, Jess. We don't mind lending it to you, but a loan is a loan."

"This wouldn't happen to Brooke Shields," Jessica said, infuriated.

"Not to mention," Mrs. Wakefield continued mildly, "the sixty-seven-dollar bill that just came from Lisette's."

Jessica's eyes flashed with indignation. "I'll pay it back—every penny. I'll even give you interest," she added, injured.

Mr. Wakefield laughed. "That won't be necessary, Jess. We figure you're a pretty worthwhile investment."

Jessica's anger was beginning to diminish in her excitement about the job. "You won't regret it," she said enthusiastically. "Will you come to Lytton and Brown and watch me?"

"Of course we will," Mrs. Wakefield said, patting her arm. "Honey, we'll all be thrilled if it works out for you. And we'll certainly be there to cheer you on."

"Speaking of cheering," Mr. Wakefield said, "has it occurred to any of you that the Ramsbury Fair is coming up? It happens to be the day after Jessica's fashion show."

Elizabeth's expression brightened. The Ramsbury Fair had always been one of the family's favorite outings. Ramsbury was a small town about ten miles from Sweet Valley, and everyone pitched in to make the fair special. Hayrides, a big amusement park, dozens of games, and square dancing were all featured. Elizabeth and Jessica had always gone with their parents, usually inviting a few special friends. In fact, Elizabeth had already mentioned the fair once to Jeffrey, and she had been hoping he'd come along with them that year.

"Ugh," Jessica said inelegantly. "I don't want to be rude, but don't you think Liz and I are a little old for that kind of thing now?"

Mr. Wakefield looked surprised. "Why? Your mother and I have managed to hobble along every year. And we're practically on our way to the old folks' home!"

Jessica giggled. "Oh, Daddy," she said. "You know what I mean! Those dumb hayrides and everything." She wrinkled her nose at the memory. The Ramsbury Fair might have been fun for Jessica Wakefield, but not for Jessa Fields. "Count me out this time," she added, bouncing up from the table.

"Jess, you haven't eaten a thing," Mrs. Wakefield pointed out.

"I have to watch my weight!" Jessica called over her shoulder as she hurried from the room.

Elizabeth stared at her plate. She kept hoping that Jessica would snap out of it, but it looked as though the new image was here to stay. She knew she should be happy for Jessica about her new modeling career. And maybe Jessica was right—maybe the fair was too childish for them now.

But then why did she feel so lonesome? Why did it seem to her that she and Jessica had lost something precious, something they were in danger of never being able to recover?

Seven

"Liz!" Jeffrey called, a hint of impatience in his voice. "I've been chasing you all the way down this hall," he complained a minute later, huffing a little as he caught up to her. "Have you been purposely avoiding me, or is it just getting harder to get hold of you?"

Elizabeth was quiet for a moment. It was true. She *had* been avoiding Jeffrey. He had called the night before, and she told her mother she was in the bathtub. "I was going to call you back last night, but—"

"Never mind," Jeffrey said, leaning over to give her a quick kiss on the cheek. "I only wanted to make sure you still wanted to see that new movie tonight."

Elizabeth didn't answer right away. If only she

knew what to do about Jeffrey! She liked him so much. But that was the problem. If she was headed for heartache, she would prefer to call things off now, before she was in even deeper.

"In fact, we've got an awful lot of planning to do," Jeffrey said. "One of the reasons I was calling last night, aside from checking to see about tonight, was that I wanted to ask you if my cousin Bryce could come along to that fair you were telling me about in Ramsbury. It turns out he's going to be visiting from Oregon that weekend, and I thought it might be nice to bring him with us."

"Oh, *that*," Elizabeth said disparagingly. "I'm not really sure I want to go to the fair that much after all, Jeffrey."

"Why not?" he asked, walking along beside her as they headed to the cafeteria. "I thought you said it was always so much fun."

"Well, it always *used* to be," Elizabeth said halfheartedly. "But I don't know. . . . Jessica says she thinks she's too grown-up for it this year. And I'm just not sure it'll be any fun without her."

Jeffrey's mouth tightened a little. He seemed to be thinking very hard and fast about something. "Fine," he said shortly. "I didn't really want to go much anyway."

Elizabeth stared at him. "You just changed your mind because of Jessica," she said accusingly. "You were perfectly willing to go until I told you what she said."

Jeffrey's green eyes flashed with anger. "Yeah, that's right," he said sarcastically. "If Jessica can't go, then why should we go? Why shouldn't we decide everything we do on the basis of Jessica?"

Elizabeth felt her face burn. "I'm beginning to get the picture," she said coldly. "You just—"

"Liz," Jeffrey pleaded, the sarcasm dropping from his voice, "don't you realize—"

"I realize perfectly well," Elizabeth interrupted, "that you don't really feel like going to the fair now that Jessica isn't going." She glared at him, her anger mounting. "I guess there isn't really much reason for us to go see a movie tonight, since Jessica has other plans."

"Liz, what are you talking about?" Jeffrey demanded, grabbing her arm as she started to stalk off.

Elizabeth felt her eyes fill with angry tears. "Why don't you just ask Jessica to go out with you?" she muttered, edging away from him.

"I'm not going to just stand here and let you make a complete fool out of me!" Jeffrey exploded. "If you want to break our date tonight, why don't you just come up with some kind of decent excuse—like tell me you're going to be taking a bath again or something!"

Jeffrey's voice had risen, and various students turned to look in the couple's direction.

"Fine," Elizabeth seethed, ignoring the stares of passersby. "That's just what I will do. Because I'm not going out with you tonight, that's for sure!" With that she stormed off, tears spilling over and running down her cheeks.

She couldn't believe Jeffrey had done this to her. Couldn't he at least have covered up his disappointment when she told him Jessica didn't want to go to Ramsbury this year? Did he have to make it so patently obvious that Jessica was the one he had his heart set on?

Elizabeth couldn't wait for the day to end. She felt as if her whole world were falling apart. First she had lost her twin sister. Then her diary. And now it looked as if she had lost Jeffrey French as well.

"Where are you going tonight?" Elizabeth asked her sister as she threw herself across Jessica's bed.

Jessica was standing in front of her mirror, holding her dark hair back from her face. "Lila and I are going to the Beach Disco. What about you? Aren't you going out with Jeffrey?"

Elizabeth sighed heavily. "You sure look nice in those pants," she said, watching Jessica pivot in the black leather jeans. No wonder Jeffrey admired her so much. Who could blame him?

Jessica didn't seem to notice her twin hadn't answered her question. "Don't I?" she agreed happily. "You know, I'm thinking of doing something really drastic to my hair after the fashion show at Lytton and Brown. I was talking to Jim, Mr. Avery's assistant, about it today when I had my pictures taken. He thinks something really short and sleek—not punk, but definitely more contemporary than just this long hanging stuff."

Elizabeth didn't respond. *Great*, she was thinking. *The last thing we have in common is long hair—and now Jessica wants to chop hers off!*

"Jim thinks I need something interesting, something with dimension. You know, a kind of geometric cut," Jessica continued.

"Jim seems pretty interested in you," Elizabeth observed.

"Well, he likes my look," Jessica said modestly.

"He isn't the only one." Elizabeth sighed. "Jess, do you realize that everyone has talked about nothing else since you went to Lila's and transformed yourself?"

Jessica looked at her sister with genuine delight. "Really? What have people been saying?"

"Oh, you know, just that you look absolutely

great with dark hair, that you look so sleek and sophisticated, that your new clothes are out of this world. That sort of thing."

Jessica chuckled happily. "Well, well, well," she crooned, turning back to the mirror and putting some crimson lipstick on. Catching sight of her sister's downcast expression behind her in the mirror, she raised her eyebrows quizzically. "Liz, you're not upset about anything, are you?"

Elizabeth sighed heavily. "Well . . ."

Jessica's eyes darkened. Deep down she couldn't bear the thought of her sister's being upset about anything. "Tell me," she begged. "You look so sad!"

Elizabeth shrugged. "I—I don't know, I guess I miss the way it used to be. When you and I looked pretty much alike."

Jessica looked immeasurably relieved. "Oh, is that all?" she said, returning to her lipstick.

Elizabeth bit her lip. "Well, don't you? I mean, honestly, Jess, don't you miss going places and having people make a fuss because we look identical?"

"Nope," Jessica said, blotting her lipstick with a bit of tissue. "Liz, can't you see how much better it is this way—for both of us?"

Elizabeth stared at her, unconvinced.

"No, I mean it," Jessica said earnestly. "Listen, I read this whole study in a magazine recently. Supposedly twins have a real identity crisis at some point. The guy who wrote this article seemed to think that distinguishing characteristics were the best idea."

Elizabeth shook her head, her blond hair tumbling around her shoulders. "But we always looked different," she reminded Jessica. "You wore different clothes than I did. All the people who mattered could tell us apart."

"Ha!" Jessica said with a snort. "Well, then why did Jeffrey mistake me for you the day I wore that dress Grandma sent you?"

Elizabeth stared at her incredulously. "I hope that didn't have anything to do with this," she said bitterly.

"Well, you can see how it would be a little disturbing, can't you? I mean, I used to think the same way you do. But when my twin's own *boyfriend* mistakes me for her . . ."

Elizabeth took a deep breath. "Wow," she said finally. "The irony of the whole thing is pretty amazing."

"Irony? What are you talking about?"

"Well, just that it seems pretty funny that you decided to dye your hair and everything because Jeffrey got us mixed up. He sure seems to like the results."

"What are you talking about?" Jessica demanded, putting her lipstick down.

As Elizabeth got to her feet, her eyes filled

with tears. "He's just one of your biggest fans all of a sudden, that's all."

"Jeffrey? *Your* Jeffrey?" Jessica's voice was getting higher and higher.

Elizabeth nodded. "I guess once he could tell the difference between us, it was easier for him to decide whom he preferred," she said, heading to the door.

Jessica's eyes were as wide as saucers. "Liz, are you sure you aren't making some kind of mistake? Jeffrey's crazy about you. Any idiot could see that!"

"Well, I hate to disagree with the idiot point of view," Elizabeth said sarcastically, her unhappiness getting the better of her, "but the fact is, I think he likes you, Jess."

"Does that mean you're not going to see him tonight?" Jessica asked, looking very confused.

Elizabeth nodded, trying hard to look as though she didn't care. "As far as I'm concerned, we just may never speak to each other again," she said, closing the door behind her and ignoring her twin's expression of stupefaction.

"Wow," Lila said when Jessica had finished recounting the conversation she and Elizabeth had had. "It sure sounds like they're on the rocks, Jess."

"I'm only telling you because I thought you'd

be overjoyed," Jessica pointed out. "Now I guess you can make another attempt for him."

Lila looked hurt. "No, thanks," she said dryly. "I've already humiliated myself enough over him. You think I'm going to start chasing him again when he made it perfectly clear he wasn't one bit interested in me? Besides," she added, taking a sip of her soda and looking across the crowded floor of the Beach Disco to a table of cute guys, "I happen to have other ideas. Don't you think Gregg McGinnis is cute?"

Jessica didn't answer. She was stirring her Coke with her straw and thinking about Jeffrey French.

"Anyway, *you're* the one who ought to go after him. Didn't Liz say he thought you looked terrific now?"

Jessica looked thoughtfully at her friend. "You know, Lila, you may have a point. Can you really see Jeffrey and me together?"

Lila shrugged. "I don't see why not," she said. "I'm going to go ask Gregg to dance," she added, pushing her chair back and getting up from the table.

Jessica barely noticed her go. She turned her drink around and around on the table, making little wet rings on the wood.

She had always thought Jeffrey was kind of cute. And if what Elizabeth said was true—if he really did have a crush on her . . .

Jessica didn't want her sister to feel bad. But it was perfectly clear that Elizabeth was finished with Jeffrey.

So maybe it wouldn't be the end of the world if Jessica tried to get to know him a little better.

Eight

Jessica got dressed for school on Monday morning with unusual care, even for the new Jessica. "Jessa Fields," she murmured, smoothing the sleek gray trousers down with one hand as she selected a cherry-red blouse and a lightweight, man-tailored gray jacket. She wanted to look perfect that day. In the first place, she had an appointment with Simon Avery after school, and Richard Mahler would have made his decision by then about the fashion show. Jessica felt certain that she had the job, but it wouldn't hurt to look her best. She applied even more makeup that morning, insuring that the glamorous look that had so impressed Simon Avery would make an even stronger impression on Richard Mahler.

And Jeffrey French.

All weekend Jessica had been thinking about Jeffrey, and by now she felt sure that there was only one thing to do—confront Jeffrey, and see if there was any truth in what Elizabeth had told her.

Not that she saw any reason to doubt it, especially the way Elizabeth had been moping around the house all weekend, stone faced and sullen. Jessica couldn't remember ever seeing her sister so depressed. Nothing Jessica could say or do did anything to cheer her, not that Jessica had much time to devote to the project. She was too busy shopping with Lila for clothes for "Jessa Fields." Jessica was certain that once her modeling career got off the ground she was going to need a whole new wardrobe.

"Jess, can you meet me right after school?" Elizabeth asked when Jessica had parked the twins' red Fiat convertible in the lot next to Sweet Valley High. "I promised Mom I'd be home early. She has a bunch of stuff she wants me to do for her."

"Sure," Jessica said gaily, turning off the engine and hopping out of the car. She didn't bother telling Elizabeth they would have to make a stop on the way home. She knew that Elizabeth was bound to be crabby about Mr. Avery and the whole modeling concept. It was better to wait and tell her when they were driving home.

Besides, Jessica was in a hurry. She wanted to find Jeffrey French.

Sighing, Elizabeth watched her twin bound off. She couldn't remember a Monday morning that had felt this dreary to her. It seemed as if there was nothing to look forward to. Jeffrey hadn't called all weekend, and by now her worst fears were confirmed. If he hadn't had a crush on Jessica after all, wouldn't he have called to apologize?

Elizabeth stopped by the *Oracle* office on her way to the locker, glancing, as always, to the spot on her desk where she had placed her diary. Of course it wasn't there. The note she and Mr. Collins had put on the bulletin board in the office obviously hadn't helped.

"I guess our note isn't working yet," a voice behind her said gently.

Elizabeth jumped about a mile. "Hi, Mr. Collins," she said, trying to force a smile and not succeeding. "I guess it hasn't," she agreed. "Truthfully, I'm beginning to give up on it."

"That doesn't sound like Elizabeth Wakefield," Mr. Collins said, putting his hand on her shoulder. "Hey," he added, looking at her more closely, "is something the matter?"

"Just the Monday-morning blues," Elizabeth said slowly. She didn't see any point in burdening Mr. Collins with the truth—that it wasn't the Monday-morning blues at all.

The truth was, Elizabeth was lonesome and sad. She missed Jessica. She missed having a twin to confide in—and a journal to pour her heart out to. And most of all she missed Jeffrey French.

"Jeffrey!" Jessica called gaily, waving her arm in the air like a flag. Jeffrey looked up from the table where he was eating lunch alone and smiled briefly at her.

"Don't move. I'm coming over!" Jessica called, hurrying toward him with her tray.

"Hi, Jess," Jeffrey said, pushing his tray aside.

As she sat down, Jessica inspected him carefully from lowered lashes. He didn't look well, she decided. Kind of tired and pale, as if he hadn't been sleeping much. *He must really be crazy about me*, she thought happily, *if he's losing sleep.*

"I've been looking for you everywhere," she said huskily, putting her hand meaningfully on his arm and staring into his eyes.

Jeffrey blinked and looked at her a little strangely. "Really?" he asked. "Why?"

Jessica smiled knowingly at him. Jeffrey was playing hard to get, she thought, but she didn't mind a bit. "Jeffrey, I think the two of us need to get to know each other a lot better," she said suggestively. "Don't you think I'm right?"

"I guess so," he said, staring dully at his untouched lunch.

"Aren't you hungry?" Jessica asked solicitously. "You have to eat, Jeffrey."

"I just don't feel like food today," he muttered listlessly.

"I'm not hungry, either," Jessica lied. Actually her stomach was growling loudly, and she had a sudden overwhelming desire for something substantial to eat. Then and there she decided her diet was going to have to go. "I'm going to get some more food," she told him. "Maybe we'll both feel like eating if we get something appetizing to eat."

A few minutes later she was back, her tray heaped with french fries and ice cream. Jeffrey gave her a strange look as she began to eat, but Jessica shrugged it off. "I don't know what it is about you, Jeffrey," Jessica said and gave him a radiant smile. "You just make me feel so much better. My appetite is back!"

"Hey, Jess, has Liz said anything to you about me?" he demanded suddenly, a strange, intense expression in his eyes.

Jessica blinked. This wasn't the turn she was hoping the conversation would take. "Not really," she said delicately, unwrapping an ice cream sandwich. "Why do you ask?"

"I don't know," he said morosely, watching

her eat. "It's the weirdest thing. One minute everything was great, and the next—"

"These things happen," Jessica said philosophically. "It's all part of the magic. When someone else comes along—"

"I don't want anyone else," Jeffrey said miserably. "That's the terrible thing, Jess. I'm nuts about your sister. I just wish I could figure out why she started acting so bizarre all of a sudden."

Jessica stared. Something had definitely gotten mixed up here. How had Elizabeth gotten the idea that Jeffrey was interested in *her*? Was it possible her twin was not only blind and deaf, but completely senseless as well?

Suddenly it occurred to Jessica that she had just come very close to making a fool of herself. "Oh, there's Lila," she said suddenly, standing up and grabbing her tray. "See you later, Jeffrey." She swept away with all the dignity she could muster under the circumstances, swearing at her sister under her breath.

She couldn't believe Elizabeth had played such a dirty trick. Well, Jessica was going to butt out of the whole thing now. Elizabeth and Jeffrey would have to muddle through on their own. Jessica wasn't going to help them repair their little lovers' tiff, that much was certain!

*   *   *

"Jess, why didn't you tell me we'd have to stop at the photographer's? I could have taken the bus," Elizabeth said.

Jessica was in no mood for Elizabeth's complaints just then. "Liz, this is the biggest moment in my entire life," she pointed out, pulling the Fiat into the lot in front of Simon Avery's office. "Come on," she added. "I need you for moral support."

"Oh, all right." Elizabeth sighed. Sometimes she felt as though Jessica could get away with murder—and this was one of those times. But now that they were there she didn't see any point in sitting in the car and sulking. Maybe there would be a magazine to read in the waiting room.

Once inside, Elizabeth refused to go a step farther than the waiting room. She had no interest in meeting Simon Avery *or* in hearing about her sister's fantastic new image. In fact that was the last thing she wanted to talk about or hear about just then.

So Jessica went in to see Mr. Avery alone, and Elizabeth waited in the reception area. "Does it always take this long?" she asked the receptionist twenty minutes later.

The receptionist frowned at the clock. "Mr. Mahler is in there with them," she said. "Maybe they're discussing the fashion show."

"I don't understand," Elizabeth said. "Who's Mr. Mahler?"

"The art director for Lytton and Brown," the receptionist explained.

Elizabeth was about to ask another question when the door burst open and Jessica came out, her eyes looking red and puffy and her face streaked as if she had been crying. A slender man wearing horn-rimmed glasses kept patting her consolingly on the shoulder. He was followed by a heavyset man in a gray suit who seemed slightly embarrassed by the scene.

"Come on, Liz," Jessica said, coming over to scoop up the books she had left lying on the couch. "They don't want me. They think my image is all wrong."

Elizabeth felt a wave of sympathy for her sister. She had never really seen the appeal of modeling, but she knew Jessica had truly wanted this fashion-show job. She also knew Jessica would be deeply in debt to her parents without it.

"I think we should talk about this further," Simon Avery said, kneading his fingers and looking at Mr. Mahler with concern.

But Mr. Mahler didn't hear him. He was staring at Elizabeth, his eyes widening. The next minute he snapped his fingers and smiled.

"That's it!" he cried, pointing at Elizabeth. "She's exactly who I'm looking for!"

"But I really look just like her," Jessica insisted. The four of them were seated in Mr. Avery's office, and Jessica was trying to explain what had happened. "See, we're twins," she told Mr. Mahler. "But I got tired of looking exactly like Elizabeth, so I thought I'd change my image."

Mr. Mahler looked at her closely. "I'm sorry," he said, shaking his head. "I just can't believe it. You two don't look anything alike. Your features are similar, but aside from that . . ."

Jessica felt her eyes fill with tears of frustration. "Tell them, Lizzie," she begged. "Tell them we're identical twins."

"She's right," Elizabeth said obligingly. "We are."

Mr. Mahler leaned forward and looked hard at Elizabeth. "Young lady, I'm willing to pay you six hundred dollars if you'll do the show for us. That's a hundred dollars more than we'd originally planned. What do you say?"

Elizabeth shook her head reluctantly. "I just don't—"

"Wait!" Mr. Mahler exclaimed, putting up his hand. "Don't decide one way or another yet. You obviously need time to think about it. Why don't you go home, get a good night's sleep, and come in and let us know tomorrow."

"I'm not sure that's really necessary," Elizabeth objected.

Jessica listened in disbelief. "*I* could do it," she insisted. "Honestly, if I just wash this stuff out of my hair and take off all this makeup . . ."

Mr. Mahler shook his head at her. "You see, we really want someone fresh faced. Someone original. Your look is fine, but it's much too unconventional and stylized for us. So I'm afraid—"

"Why don't you both go home and think this over," Mr. Avery said.

"I don't want to think it over. I don't really want to model," Elizabeth insisted.

But Mr. Mahler refused to take no for an answer. "I think this is too big a decision to make lightly. That's why I'm not going to let you turn me down this afternoon. Go home, think it over, talk to your parents, and come back tomorrow afternoon. I'm sure you'll realize by then what a wonderful opportunity this is." His eyes were fixed intently on her face.

Elizabeth didn't see the point in arguing. "OK," she said finally, getting up.

"There's no way I'm going to be in that fashion show, Jess!" Elizabeth said as the twins were driving home. "I can't do something like that."

Jessica didn't answer. She was staring grimly

at the road in front of her, going over the scene that had just taken place.

She still couldn't believe it. How in the world could Mr. Mahler have preferred Elizabeth's scrubbed, sunny looks to her own sophisticated new image? What had happened to the start of Jessa Fields' career?

Jessica felt like crying. She had been so certain Mr. Mahler was going to choose her. And instead he'd said she was too unconventional and stylized for them! She felt as though he had slapped her. It was too unfair. Too unspeakably unfair.

But Jessica wasn't going to take it lying down. She was going to make them change their minds—or come up with some way to be in that fashion show, no matter what!

Nine

That night at dinner neither Jessica nor Elizabeth had very much to say. Elizabeth was withdrawn and thoughtful, mulling over the events of the last several days and thinking about how much she missed Jeffrey. Jessica was a million miles away, upset about what had happened at the photographer's office, worried about the money she owed her parents, and trying to think of a way to change Mr. Mahler's mind the following day.

"Is it my imagination, or is it unusually quiet around here tonight?" Mr. Wakefield asked his wife.

Mrs. Wakefield smiled at him. "Maybe we should just enjoy it while it lasts," she suggested. "Girls," she added, "your father and I are trying to splice together some old home movies to send to Grandma and Grandpa. Do you think you could help us pick the best ones to send them?"

"Sure," Elizabeth said automatically, wishing she felt more enthusiastic about the prospect. "In fact, why don't I go start setting up the projector? I'm really not very hungry."

Mrs. Wakefield looked concerned. "Are you feeling all right?" she asked, putting her hand on Elizabeth's forehead to check for fever.

Elizabeth nodded. "I'm fine," she said, getting up from the table.

Mrs. Wakefield looked inquisitively at Jessica. "Do you know what's bugging your sister?" she asked as Elizabeth went down to the basement to look for the projector.

Jessica shook her head. "She's probably just tired," she said, feeling a tiny twinge of guilt as she remembered the conversation she and Jeffrey had had at lunch. She knew she should tell Elizabeth what he had said about her, but somehow Jessica just couldn't bring herself to help her sister and Jeffrey get back together again. It seemed too insulting after the humiliation she had been through.

Besides, Jessica was too absorbed with her own problem to worry about Elizabeth. It seemed to her that there was only one logical way out of the mess she had gotten herself into.

That was to transform herself back into the old Jessica Wakefield in time to convince Mr. Mahler that she was really Elizabeth. And that she wanted the modeling job after all.

Jessica kept turning this over and over in her mind. The problem was that she would have to admit she had made a mistake. Hadn't she told everyone that the new image was around for good? And, besides, she would look exactly like Elizabeth again—a bonus as far as the Lytton and Brown job went, but the same old problem apart from that. Jessica felt that she had worked so hard to establish a separate identity. Was it really worth sacrificing that for the modeling job?

"You know," her mother was saying, looking at her meaningfully, "since Liz is busy setting up the projector, Jess, the dishes—"

Jessica jumped to her feet, her hand cupped over one ear. "I think someone's at the door," she explained, hurrying from the room before her mother's request became too specific to easily ignore.

"Jess!" she heard her mother calling after her. But just then the door bell did ring.

"I'll be back in a second!" Jessica called back, opening the front door and looking with some surprise into the concerned face of Penny Ayala. "Hi, Penny! Come on in," she said, opening the door wider and smiling at the attractive, brown-haired senior.

Penny shook her head regretfully. "I can't. My mom's in the car, waiting for me," she explained. "Jess, I feel just awful. Will you tell Liz I had no idea her journal was under the pile of stuff I moved last week?"

"Her journal?" Jessica repeated blankly. "What are you talking about?"

"Mr. Collins has been helping her look for it," Penny explained breathlessly, "and apparently she's been absolutely frantic about it. I can imagine if I lost *my* diary . . ."

Jessica stared at the black-and-white composition book Penny was handing her. Sure enough, it seemed to be her sister's journal. And Jessica hadn't even known it was lost! Staring down at the notebook, Jessica felt strangely sad. It occurred to her that she and Elizabeth had barely been keeping up with each other's lives lately. She couldn't remember the last time she had felt so distant from her sister.

"Anyway, I had to pick some stuff up in the office today, and I saw her note on the bulletin board," Penny explained hastily. "I hadn't even known it was missing! But right away I realized what must've happened. And sure enough, the notebook had been moved into the storage room. It was there all along."

"Thanks, Penny," Jessica said slowly, turning the composition book over in her hands. "I'll give it to her right away."

"Tell her how sorry I am," Penny begged, waving her hand at her mother to show her she was coming in a second. "I'll find her at school tomorrow to apologize in person."

"OK—and thanks again," Jessica said absently, closing the door after Penny and looking thoughtfully at her sister's journal.

Suddenly Jessica had an almost overwhelming desire to look at the journal. She knew Elizabeth would kill her, but the sense that she and her twin had grown apart was so strong that she felt justified opening the notebook and flipping through the pages. She could hear Elizabeth moving around down in the basement, and Jessica knew she was, for the moment, perfectly safe.

Within seconds Jessica's guilt had evaporated as she became absorbed in her sister's writing. Most of the recent entries seemed to be about Jeffrey and her feelings for him. Then Jessica came to a passage that caught her eye:

I'm sure I'm overreacting, but looking at Jessica now is incredibly painful for me. It isn't that she doesn't look fantastic— because she does! What hurts is that she doesn't look like part of *us* anymore. This whole thing has made me think very hard about what it means to be a twin. And I guess it's much more important to me than I ever realized. Being a twin isn't just looking the same, though that part (for me, at least) was always fun.

I guess for me being a twin has to do with being unusually close. It means knowing what Jessica is thinking and feeling even when no one else does. And it means she knows me better than anyone else in the whole world.

Well, that's what I'm finding hardest about Jessica's new image. Not that she looks different so much, but that she's shutting me out. If only she knew how much I cared for her and if only she understood that looking identical has never kept us from having distinct identities! Maybe I could have told the old Jessica how I felt. But the new Jessica is like a stranger to me.

"Jess? Who was at the door?" Mrs. Wakefield called from the kitchen. Jessica blinked guiltily and closed the notebook.

"It was Penny Ayala, dropping off something for Liz," she called back. She knew she had to take the journal down to Elizabeth right away.

She couldn't have read another line anyway. Her eyes were blurred with tears, and she had to take several deep breaths to control herself before descending the stairs to meet her sister.

A half hour later the Wakefields were curled up on the soft couches in the living room, completely absorbed in watching old home movies.

"Look at me. I look so young!" Mrs. Wakefield cried, putting her hands up to her face as she watched herself on the screen fussing over the twins, aged six.

"You still look pretty good to me," Mr. Wakefield said affectionately, giving her a warm hug.

"Jess, remember those dresses?" Elizabeth asked, then groaned. "Mom, why in the world did you let us wear those red things? We look like tomatoes!"

"You just happen to have been the cutest things in the entire world," her mother informed her. "Look, there we all are the first year we went to the Ramsbury Fair!"

Jessica felt a weird sensation in the pit of her stomach as she watched herself and her sister on the screen sitting in the back of a pickup truck covered with hay.

"I don't think we understood what a hayride was then." Elizabeth laughed. "We seemed to think it meant riding around with all the hay on top of us!"

"Still, we had a really good time," Jessica

pointed out. "Liz, maybe we *should* go this year," she said, putting her hand on her sister's arm.

Elizabeth gave her a funny look. "I thought all that was 'kid stuff' now," she objected.

Jessica stared at the image of the two tiny blond girls holding hands in all that hay. She had to admit that they looked adorable. They were dressed exactly alike in little denim overalls and plaid shirts, but even so, Jessica knew right away which little girl was she and which was Elizabeth. *Liz is right,* she thought, getting a little misty-eyed. *We may look the same, but we're two completely separate people.*

"It isn't kid stuff," she said in a low voice. "Liz, I'd like to go. Am I too late, or are you still interested?"

Elizabeth looked at her earnestly. The next minute a huge smile broke over her face. "Of course you're not too late!" she exclaimed.

Jessica grinned at her. "Hey, maybe we can even dig up matching clothes," she suggested. "Like we did the first year we went."

"No, thanks!" Elizabeth said and laughed. "No offense, Jess, but I think I'm going to leave the leather jeans and high heels to you. *I* prefer dressing like a normal person."

"Hey, what are you two talking about over there?" Mr. Wakefield asked. "You're supposed to be helping us edit this masterpiece we're making."

Soon the twins were mesmerized again. "I don't remember your taking movies of this!" Elizabeth wailed, covering her eyes as the twins, aged eleven, flashed on the screen in Halloween costumes—Elizabeth and Amy Sutton dressed as clowns, and Jessica and Lila as hula dancers. "God, would you look at Amy," Elizabeth added, giggling. Her former best friend had moved away at the end of the sixth grade, but she had just returned to Sweet Valley. In the time Amy had been gone, her personality had changed drastically. Now she was more Jessica's sort of person than Elizabeth's.

"Oh, no!" Jessica moaned as the next image came on screen—the twins at their commencement exercises from middle school, dressed in identical white gowns, hugging each other and giggling. "Daddy, we look too weird in those gowns. Don't send those to Grandma and Grandpa!"

"OK, but this one is a must," Mr. Wakefield said. The twins were dressed in ski clothes, and Steven was behind them pretending to push them down the bunny hill. It had been their first ski lesson, and having an older brother who was already an expert had proved to be more of a pain than a help!

Jessica felt conflicting emotions as she

105

watched the home movies. On the one hand she didn't want them to end. But suddenly she felt that there was so much she wanted to talk to Elizabeth about.

First and foremost, she wanted to tell her about her talk with Jeffrey. Jessica could see now how petty and selfish she was being, keeping the exchange to herself. She wasn't sure what had gone wrong between her twin and Jeffrey, but now she wanted to help them if she could.

Jessica felt as though she had a million things to think about. And tops on the list was how she was going to get every bit of the black dye out of her hair in time to impersonate Elizabeth the next afternoon and take over her modeling job at Lytton and Brown!

Ten

"I don't believe it," Elizabeth said slowly, sitting on the edge of her bed, watching Jessica scrub the makeup off her face with tissues and cold cream. "You mean Jeffrey really acted like he missed me?"

"Missed you?" Jessica snorted. "Liz, the guy is nuts about you." She shook her head, remembering her humiliation now with great amusement. "In fact, he barely even seemed to notice who I was or to hear what I was saying. He just wanted to pump me for information about you."

"It's incredible," Elizabeth murmured, half to herself. "All week I've been feeling sorry for myself because I felt I was out of a diary, a boyfriend—"

"And a twin sister," Jessica filled in for her,

backing up to inspect herself now that the makeup was off. "Now I think I need a really good shampoo," she muttered, wrinkling her nose as she regarded the dark hair cascading around her shoulders. "I'm still not convinced blondes have more fun, but if Mr. Mahler wants a blonde, then he's going to get one," she declared, stomping off toward the bathroom with her towel in hand.

"Jessica!" Elizabeth shrieked, bouncing off the bed. "You mean you're changing yourself back to being a plain old boring Wakefield twin?" She could hardly believe how wonderful everything was all of a sudden.

Jessica gave her a wry look. "Don't count on it," she said, sounding more like the old Jessica with each syllable. "When, may I ask, was being a Wakefield twin ever boring? Or *plain*?"

Elizabeth threw her arms around her twin, hugging her so hard Jessica yelped with pain. "Hey," she said, disentangling herself. "Anyway, I don't have much choice," she called over her shoulder as she trotted toward the shower. "If I don't convince Mr. Mahler that I'm you by tomorrow afternoon, I'm going to be in debt to Mom and Dad for the rest of my life!"

Elizabeth could hardly believe it. First Penny had brought back her journal, apparently unharmed—and unread! And now it looked as

108

though Jessica was going to change back into Jessica.

Best of all, it sounded as if Jeffrey hadn't been in love with Jessica at all. Elizabeth was sure there would still be a lot of explaining they would each have to do, but at least there was hope.

She could hardly wait to see Jeffrey in school the next morning. She would be more than happy to explain everything if there was the slightest chance of getting back together with him again.

Elizabeth couldn't sleep. She had so many things to think about, and the longer she lay in bed the more active and awake she felt. The house was perfectly quiet, but finally Elizabeth gave up. Since she couldn't sleep, she might as well take advantage of being awake! she decided.

Slipping into her robe and picking up her journal, she padded barefoot out into the hallway and slipped quietly down the carpeted stairs. The house was completely transformed in the moonlight; everything was so silvery and pretty, she thought. Setting her journal down on the kitchen table, Elizabeth crossed to the refrigerator and began to fix herself a midnight snack. She realized that she hadn't had much to eat at dinner, and suddenly she was ravenous. Equipping herself with a big red apple and a jar of peanut butter, she sat down at the kitchen table, sliced the apple, and began to spread each slice thick with peanut butter. As she ate she stared out at the moonlit yard, thinking over the events of the evening. She got goose bumps just thinking about Jeffrey. So he hadn't liked Jessica after all. . . . She couldn't wait until morning, when she could see him again and maybe, just maybe, they could make up. She felt all tingly thinking about talking to him. "What a dope I've been," she murmured, biting into another peanut-buttery slice of apple.

When she had finished her snack and gotten herself a glass of cold milk to quench her thirst, Elizabeth picked her journal up. What an incredible relief it was to have it back again! she thought. She couldn't believe it had just been down in storage all the time. Thank heavens Penny had realized what had happened. Now that the journal was recovered, Elizabeth could admit how terribly worried she had been since she had misplaced it. The thought of anyone reading any of the personal entries she had written made her cringe.

But now it was back! And what joy it was to pick up a brand new pen and turn to a new page. Chewing on the end of her pen and looking out at the silvery trees, Elizabeth felt a wave of contentment wash over her. She began to write.

I don't know where to begin. So many things have happened since I thought I lost this book! I guess most of them are pretty good things. At least tonight they seem good. For one thing, Jessica is going to turn back into herself.

Now that she's back to the old Jessica, I think I can honestly say that her making herself over was one of the worst things that's ever happened to me. Maybe I reacted too strongly, but I think it almost broke my heart to look at her and see a stranger's face—and hear a stranger's voice!

I've never been able to clearly sort out how I feel about being "one of a pair," as Jessica would put it, until this. I guess I realized these past few weeks that it means much more to me than I thought. Because it hurt me so much once that special relationship seemed threatened.

And speaking of special relationships, I still can't believe everything that's gone on this week with Jeffrey and me. I can't believe how close we've come to losing each other. When I think about him tonight I feel really strange—half excited, as if something wonderful might happen, and half scared, in case it doesn't. What if it's too late?

Elizabeth sighed and closed her journal. If only the night would hurry up and be over! Then she could get dressed, hurry to school, and he'd be there.

She knew she was going to have to be patient, but right now she felt that that was impossible. She couldn't wait for it to be morning.

She just had to know that Jeffrey was willing to talk things through with her, willing, as she was, to give their relationship another chance!

"Hey," Elizabeth said, crossing the soft grassy lawn toward Jeffrey, who was sitting under a tree in front of the school and staring absent-mindedly into space. An uneaten sandwich, still wrapped in wax paper, lay beside him on a brown paper bag. "Are you busy, or could you stand some company?"

Jeffrey stared at her, his eyes brightening. Then his face fell. "I guess I'm not busy," he mumbled.

"Jeffrey, I want to talk—really talk," Elizabeth said, dropping down beside him and facing him. "I feel as though I've been acting like a prize idiot these last few days. What do you think? You think we can try to talk things out?"

"I sure hope so," Jeffrey said sincerely. "I don't know how you've been feeling, Liz, but

112

I've really missed you. And I've acted like a jerk, too. Don't give yourself all the credit," he added.

Elizabeth shook her head. "Jeffrey, you're never going to believe what I thought." She began to explain how upset she had been about Jessica's transformation. "I think I was insecure about it, but even so. . . . Every time it came up, you seemed to have nothing but compliments for her. And I convinced myself you thought—that you—" But Elizabeth found she couldn't actually bring herself to tell Jeffrey what she had suspected.

Jeffrey stared at her, his face coloring. "You thought I—you mean, you thought Jessica—"

Elizabeth nodded, feeling incredibly stupid. "I just thought you preferred her new look to my old one," she whispered, staring down at the grass.

Jeffrey grabbed her hand and squeezed it tightly. "Stupid girl," he said gruffly. He made it sound like an endearment, not a reproach. "Don't you know I think you're the most beautiful girl in the world?" he demanded, tipping her chin up to stare into her eyes.

Elizabeth's voice quavered. "But, then, why . . ."

"You're not going to believe this," Jeffrey continued, "but I was having a hard time with the fact that you were a twin. It unnerved me, seeing Jessica walk past, looking like you, only not *being* you. I think when she dyed her hair and every-thing, I was incredibly relieved. I loved having you all to myself, knowing that no one looked like you anymore. *That's* why I kept harping on how good she looked."

Elizabeth burst out laughing. "Boy, we sure have been idiots." She sighed. "Jeffrey, I want to apologize. I should have trusted you, and I should've told you what I suspected instead of just blowing up at you."

"Yeah," Jeffrey said softly, stroking her hair. "Well, I should've been a little more honest myself. I was really upset when you said you didn't want to go to that fair with me just because Jessica wouldn't go! I wanted you to be satisfied with *my* company. Instead of telling you, though, I acted as if I didn't care."

Elizabeth stared at him, understanding at last. "And I thought you were trying to get out of going because *you* were disappointed that Jessica wouldn't come!" she cried, slapping her forehead.

"Listen," Jeffrey said, pulling her close to him, "I have a great idea. Let's go to the fair, just you and me. We'll have a fantastic time together."

Elizabeth smiled. "That's a great idea. But what would you say if I told you I have a feeling we might have company?"

"What do you mean?"

Elizabeth pointed. "My sister," she said

wryly, as Jessica came bounding toward them, "has suddenly decided to come to her senses. She asked me last night if she could come after all."

Jeffrey stared across the lawn. "Oh, no," he groaned with mock horror. "She looks just like you again! Just when I was getting used to being able to tell you two apart!"

"Well," Elizabeth said softly, putting her hand on his arm and smiling, "you'll just have to find some special way to differentiate us."

And pulling his face down toward hers, Elizabeth kissed him, oblivious of everything but the feel of sunlight on her bare arms and the feel of his strong arms around her.

She had a hunch Jeffrey wasn't ever going to get them confused again.

Jessica hummed to herself as she hurried down the hall. She couldn't remember the last time she had had such a good day. "Hi, Liz!" Robin Wilson exclaimed. Jessica just smiled in return.

"Elizabeth!" Mr. Collins had called that morning. "Did Penny find you? I'm so relieved your journal was just down in storage. I told you we'd find it!"

"It isn't Liz, Mr. Collins," Jessica had said

sweetly, tossing her blond hair back from her shoulders. "It's Jessica."

"Jess—" Mr. Collins had stared at her, narrowing his blue eyes. "But didn't you have—I mean, wasn't your—"

"What, Mr. Collins?" Jessica demanded, enjoying his confusion.

"Nothing," he muttered, still staring at her. "I just thought your hair was different, that's all."

Jessica giggled. "Must've just been your imagination," she told him, giving a parting wave as she hurried off again down the hall.

The best part of the day by far, though, was seeing the expression on Lila's face at lunchtime.

"Jessica? What on earth . . ." Lila gasped.

Jessica looked at her and said philosophically, "You know, the most important word as far as fashion goes is *change*, Lila. You just can't let a look get stale. You know what I mean?"

"But it hadn't been very long," Lila objected. "And we spent so much time!"

"It was very well spent," Jessica reassured her. "I just got a little sick of the whole thing. Besides, that sort of stylized, artificial look is really out now. The natural, healthy, wholesome look is in."

"Is that why you're eating all that food?" Lila demanded, studying her friend's loaded lunch tray with amusement.

116

"Wholesome," Jessica said, reaching for a chocolate chip cookie, "means that I get to gain back the three pounds I lost. And I think I'd better get to work on it right away!"

"I think you're up to something," Lila said. "You wouldn't have given up on your new image if you didn't have some kind of sneaky ulterior motive."

"Who, me?" Jessica demanded innocently, taking a big sip of chocolate milk.

She continued to stare at Lila in wide-eyed silence until her friend backed down and looked away. Jessica was enjoying herself immensely. She was getting even more attention now that people were confused about her appearance.

And if she could only convince Mr. Mahler that afternoon that she was Elizabeth, she would be starring in her very first fashion show—and earning six hundred dollars while she was at it!

Eleven

Elizabeth felt as though she were floating that entire day. "What's with you? You look like you just won the lottery," Enid joked. Elizabeth just smiled dreamily at her. She realized now how down she had been recently, because she suddenly felt as if a weight had been lifted from her.

"I take it things are OK with you and Jeffrey," Enid remarked, walking with her friend to class.

"They're more than OK," Elizabeth said blissfully. "He's such an amazingly nice guy, Enid. I was so stupid to be angry with him!"

"Hey," Enid said suddenly, grabbing Elizabeth's arm. "Am I seeing double, or has Jessica changed back into Jessica?"

Elizabeth giggled. "Isn't it wonderful?" she said, watching Jessica streak through the hallway, her blond hair flying. "Boy, I can't tell you how good it is to see her without all that makeup on."

"I didn't think she looked half-bad," Enid protested.

Elizabeth gave her a dirty look, and Enid backed down, laughing. "All right, all right," she said with mock resignation. "I agree, Liz. Thank heavens she's restored to her usual degree of gorgeousness!"

The bell rang, signaling that class would begin in two minutes, and Enid and Elizabeth separated at the end of the corridor.

Elizabeth was almost at the door of her English class when Dana Larson, the pretty blond junior who was the lead singer for The Droids, Sweet Valley High's very own rock group, called her name. "Are you ready for our quiz on Friday?" she asked, giving Elizabeth a conspiratorial grimace as they took their seats and waited for Mr. Collins to come in and get the class started.

"Not really. I'm behind on my reading," Elizabeth admitted. Actually she had a lot of homework to catch up on. She had been so worried about everything lately that her schoolwork had been slipping. But Elizabeth loved her English class and knew she could catch up.

Mr. Collins hadn't come in yet, and Elizabeth and Dana had several minutes to talk. Elizabeth wasn't very close to Dana but had always admired her. Dana impressed her as one of those remarkable people who manage to balance many different things at once. Singing for The Droids obviously took up quite a bit of time, but Dana was also a good student and had dozens of hobbies.

"Hey, wasn't your cousin visiting you and Jessica a few weeks ago?" Dana asked Elizabeth now. "Someone told me she was here for a visit."

"That's right," Elizabeth confirmed. Jenny, their fifteen-year-old first cousin from Dallas, had stayed with the Wakefields for almost two weeks. In fact, she had been a spectator in the middle of the battle being waged over Jeffrey, Elizabeth remembered. Jenny was a nice enough girl, but she could be a pain. Jessica thought she was the worst thing to have hit the twentieth century—a view compounded by the fact that their little cousin was Jessica's biggest fan. "She was on break from school and came for a short visit," Elizabeth added, wondering why Dana was bringing Jenny up now.

"The reason I asked," Dana explained, "is that my cousin Sally is going to move in with us." She fiddled with the edge of her notebook. "I just wondered if you have any advice on how to deal with problem cousins, that's all."

"Problem cousins? Is Sally a problem?" Elizabeth asked, curious.

Dana frowned and brushed her hair back from her face. "Well, I don't know. I don't think she's that bad, but my brother, Jeremy, isn't so hot on the idea. I guess it's kind of a big thing. I mean, this isn't just a visit. Sally's coming for keeps."

Elizabeth was about to ask where Sally was living now when Mr. Collins came in. He immediately began to talk about the novel they were reading.

Elizabeth glanced over at Dana, then turned to listen to Mr. Collins. It looked as though she was going to have to wait to learn more about Sally Larson.

"Hey, Liz," Jeffrey said lazily. The two of them were sprawled on the soft, grassy banks of Secca Lake, watching a sailboat curve gracefully as it left the dock. It was Tuesday afternoon, and they were celebrating their reunion by spending the last few hours of sunlight together at the lake.

"Hey, Jeffrey," Elizabeth mimicked him, running a blade of grass along his forearm.

"I was just thinking about that diary of yours," Jeffrey said playfully. "Now that you've got it back, I don't suppose you feel like reading me some of the juicy bits—some of the parts about you and me, huh?"

Elizabeth narrowed her eyes, pretending to

think it over. "Nah, I don't think so," she said finally.

"Come on," Jeffrey begged. "I'd let you read mine—if I had one, that is."

Elizabeth giggled. "Maybe I'll let you some day, but only on one condition."

"What's that?"

"Well, you have to start a diary, too. A real diary, not just something you whip off. And you have to let *me* read *yours*."

"I guess I don't really have to read it," Jeffrey said, suddenly serious. He leaned closer, cupped her face with his hands, and stared intently into her eyes. "I guess even as close as we are we both need a little privacy," he whispered. "Just promise me one thing. Promise me we'll always be this close."

Elizabeth closed her eyes, dizzy with happiness. She could smell the warm scent of freshly cut grass and the fainter aroma of the soap Jeffrey used. Then she opened her eyes and regarded him. "I promise," she said at last.

They sealed their promise with a long, lingering kiss. When they broke apart, Elizabeth regarded Jeffrey with wonder. She still couldn't believe this was happening. Just a few days ago she had been afraid that they would never speak to each other again. Now she couldn't help feeling that everything they had been through was serving to strengthen the bond between them.

For the first time she really thought this might be love—the real thing.

And she knew Jeffrey was feeling the same way. She could tell from the husky sound in his voice when he spoke, the way his eyes looked when they fixed on hers, the tender way his fingers felt as he caressed her cheek.

She had never seen him look this way before. And she knew her own expression was the same—a mixture of happiness, awe, and affection.

She knew she never wanted this moment to end. And from the look on Jeffrey's face as he bent to kiss her again, she knew he felt exactly the same way. They didn't need words; they didn't need anything.

Elizabeth knew she was never going to forget that afternoon, not as long as she lived. After all the strife and confusion of the last few weeks, she felt as if she had been put under a magic spell.

Only it wasn't magic. It was love, which was a million times more powerful and a million times better—because that meant it could last forever!

"Well, we're both absolutely delighted, Elizabeth," Mr. Mahler said, leaning back in the chair in Simon Avery's office and putting the tips of his fingers together. "I must admit I'm a little surprised, though. Yesterday you seemed so determined to have no part of the fashion show."

"Oh, *yesterday*," Jessica scoffed, tossing back her golden hair. She thought fast, sensing that neither Simon nor Mr. Mahler was completely convinced yet. "You see, I could tell how disappointed poor Jessica was," she said suddenly, twisting a lock of hair around one of her fingers.

"Ah," Mr. Mahler said, pleased. "So you were just pretending not to want to model in the show?"

"Exactly!" Jessica exclaimed. "Jessica means well, but she—well, you saw for yourself. She's got the wrong look. She's far too *stylized*."

"That's exactly how I felt," Mr. Mahler said, nodding in agreement. "You're much better suited for the job."

"I just *couldn't* promise to take the job away from my very own sister," Jessica continued. "Can't you see what a jam I was in?"

"Well, as I said, I'm delighted you've agreed to do it," Mr. Mahler said.

Jessica could hardly believe it. A week from Saturday she was really going to be modeling on the main floor of Lytton and Brown! She closed her eyes briefly, imagining how fantastic she would look in the suede pants Mr. Mahler had shown her in the catalogue. And she was sure this was just the beginning. *Jessa Fields, don't give up yet,* she told herself with a feeling of triumph.

Jessica bounced to her feet, and broke into a huge smile. Her first modeling job! She didn't feel the slightest pang over lying about her identity, either. As far as Jessica was concerned, she was a twin again. And that meant taking full advantage of being Elizabeth's mirror image!

She had no intention of letting people mistake her for Elizabeth very often. But every once in a while—such as at that very moment—being a twin seemed to Jessica like a pretty good deal.

Twelve

"Elizabeth Wakefield, what's the big idea?" Enid gasped, staring at her friend in amazement.

Elizabeth burst into giggles. She removed the dark glasses she was wearing and ran her fingers through the short, dark wig Jessica had borrowed for her from Lila, who had used it once in a school play. "I'm going incognito today," she whispered, narrowing her eyes mysteriously. When Enid just kept staring, she relented. The two were standing on the porch in front of Enid's house. Elizabeth had stopped by to pick her up on the way to the fashion show at Lytton and Brown.

"See, Jessica only got the job by pretending to be me," Elizabeth explained. "I know," she added, adjusting the wig with a grimace. "I look horrible as a brunette, right?"

"I still don't get it," Enid complained, climbing into the passenger seat of the Fiat as Elizabeth ran around to the driver's seat. "I thought you two were through acting so weird about being twins."

Elizabeth laughed. "Enid, don't you see? Mr. Mahler is going to be there. If I looked normal—I mean, the way I always do—he might figure out what's happened!"

Enid shook her head. "Isn't that thing making your head hot?"

"A little," Elizabeth admitted. "Jeffrey's going to die!" she added, grinning in advance at the thought of his reaction.

"This really is going to be fun," Enid said, her anticipation getting the better of her. "What time does it start again, two or two-thirty?"

"Two. We'd better hurry. I promised Jeffrey we'd meet him in the parking lot. He claims he gets lost the minute he steps inside a department store."

Ten minutes later Elizabeth and Enid parked the Fiat and were joining a big crowd of Sweet Valley High students who had come to witness Jessica's debut in the world of high fashion. Dozens of people had come, Elizabeth noticed with satisfaction—Winston Egbert, who'd be sure to crack jokes throughout; Olivia Davidson and Roger Patman; Roger's cousin Bruce, who had his arm around Regina Morrow's shoulder; Lila, Cara Walker, and Amy Sutton; Caroline Pearce; and Bill Chase and his girlfriend DeeDee Gordon. Dana Larson was there as well, but Elizabeth saw no sign of her cousin Sally. She must not have arrived yet, Elizabeth thought.

With Elizabeth and Jeffrey leading the way, the group made their way up to the second floor of Lytton and Brown, where the fashion show was to be held. Chairs had been set up in a huge room that was usually used for displaying sportswear but had been cleared for the occasion. A runway had been set up toward the front of the room. Elizabeth waved at her parents, who were sitting up front. She was glad for Jessica's sake that so many people had come. She thought her parents looked at her a little strangely, but in her excitement Elizabeth had forgotten about her disguise.

"I can't believe Jess is really going high fashion on us," Winston said, watching the scene with fascination. "Hey, maybe it isn't too late for me yet," he suggested, pretending to grab Elizabeth's wig.

"Winston, cut it out," Elizabeth hissed. Mr. Mahler was coming toward them!

"I'm not kidding. I really think I have a future

129

in the business," Winston insisted. And the next minute he had snatched off her wig, leaving her facing Mr. Mahler as her blond hair tumbled around her shoulders!

"Uh—uh—hello, Mr. Mahler," Elizabeth managed weakly.

"Don't worry," he said, smiling and putting out his hand to shake hers. "I already know the entire sordid story, Elizabeth. Apparently Jessica forgot one little thing when she decided to masquerade as you today. She forgot your parents were going to be here. Of course the first thing they did was to tell me how pleased they were that Jessica had worked out so well. So you can imagine how surprised I was that I had somehow managed to get one of an identical twosome!"

Winston looked chagrined. Staring down at the black wig in his hands, he asked uneasily, "I haven't gotten anyone in trouble, have I?"

Mr. Mahler laughed. "No, you haven't. As a matter of fact, Elizabeth, I have a suggestion to make. Since you and Jessica really *are* identical, how would you like to be in the show with her?"

Elizabeth stared. "You mean today? Right now?"

"Well, why not?" Mr. Mahler laughed. "It would be easy for me to get another set of clothing in the right size. You have plenty of time to put on the first outfit. Jessica's in the dressing room right now, getting ready. You could follow her movements. What do you say? I can't pay you more, but you two could split everything right down the middle."

"Well . . ." Elizabeth said uncertainly. Jeffrey winked at her, and she could tell he thought it was a great idea. "OK!" she said at last, shaking his hand firmly. "You've got yourself a twin!"

Twenty minutes later the twins were ready. "I can't believe we're doing this," Elizabeth said, studying their reflections incredulously. They were mirror images once again—but dressed in Lytton and Brown evening dresses, all glitter and sequins.

"I'm glad you're here," Jessica said, impulsively giving her sister a hug. "I don't think modeling would be half as much fun without you, Liz."

"Or half as much money," Elizabeth reminded her dryly.

"Girls? Ready?" Mr. Mahler asked, opening the curtain to the dressing room. They looked at each other and nodded.

"Let's go," Jessica said, giving her sister's hand a squeeze as they stepped out of the dressing room together.

Elizabeth smiled radiantly at her. She couldn't remember ever feeling closer to her twin. And the very best thing was knowing that Jessica felt the exact same way. They were in this together, and that was what made it so special. Taking a deep breath, she followed her sister out onto the runway, listening with disbelief to the roar of applause as the lights dimmed.

The Lytton and Brown fashion show was beginning—and she and Jessica were an enormous hit!

A half hour after the fashion show ended, Dana Larson slowly opened the front door to her house. "Anyone home?" she called uneasily. She couldn't help hoping she would have the house to herself that afternoon. Ordinarily Dana loved an opportunity to spend time with her parents and her older brother, Jeremy. But for the last few days things had been tense around the house. And she really felt like taking it easy that afternoon and not getting involved in yet another of the arguments that had become so frequent since the Larsons had made their big announcement.

Cousin Sally was coming to live with them— for good, it seemed. Dana put her jacket and books down in the front hall. Already the fun and excitement of the fashion show and the huge hit the Wakefield twins had made was beginning to fade. At first she thought no one was at home, but then she heard noises upstairs. "Dana? Is that you?" her mother called.

"Hi, Mom," Dana called back, riffling absently through the pile of mail on the front table.

"I'm just straightening things up in Jeremy's room," her mother explained, coming to the top of the stairs. "I'll be down in a minute, OK?"

"Sure," Dana said, strolling into the Larsons' comfortable, pretty family room and sinking down into an easy chair. She loved this room. It was decorated in a traditional style, but the little extra touches made it special—the needlepoint pillows her mother had made, the pretty potted plants, the framed photographs Jeremy had taken when he was out East the summer before. And the pictures of the family on the piano . . .

Dana crossed to the piano and picked up the picture of her cousin Sally. It was funny that she and her first cousin should be virtual strangers, but that was the sad truth. She had never gotten to know her cousin at all.

Now, at age seventeen, Sally was coming to live with them.

Sally had never had much of a family life. Her father, Dana's Uncle Bill, had had a drinking problem most of his adult life. Sally was the only child. Bill had left his wife and baby daughter almost thirteen years before, and shortly afterward Sally's mother remarried—and gave her baby girl to the first in a string of foster parents to look after.

Dana had always been horrified by this. She

couldn't imagine what it would feel like to be abandoned first by your father and then by your mother. It seemed disgustingly cruel. "We mustn't be judgmental," was what Mr. Larson had said three nights before, when he made the announcement to his family. "We just have to try to help Sally in whatever way we can."

Dana couldn't agree more. In fact, she couldn't understand why they hadn't invited Sally to come live with them years ago. Apparently there had been complications with the social agency that was Sally's official guardian. The very complicated case had been brought to court after court in an attempt to circumvent the custody laws Sally was involved in. Finally, after all this time, Sally had been told she could leave the foster family she was with.

Apparently it was none too soon. Dana didn't know all the details, but she understood that her cousin had suffered a great deal. Essentially she had never really had a family. The last home she had been at proved to be the worst.

And now she was coming to live with the Larsons. Dana didn't know what to think or to expect. In a way she was kind of looking forward to it. Studying Sally's pretty, slightly remote expression in the photograph, she felt a twinge of excitement. It would be like having a sister! Maybe she and Sally could do things together— listen to music, go to some movies. . . . Sally had been through so many moves in the past few years that, although she was a year older than Dana, she would be placed in the junior class at Sweet Valley High. Dana would be able to introduce her to everyone, show her around the school . . .

The problem was Jeremy. For some reason Jeremy didn't seem very enthused about the idea of Sally's moving in. In fact, he was being awful about it. The night Mr. Larson announced that Sally was coming, Jeremy had jumped up from the table, his face contorted with emotion. "Why do we have to let her move in with us? Can't someone else take her in?"

"Jeremy!" Mrs. Larson had gasped, appalled.

"This girl is part of our family, Jeremy," Mr. Larson said calmly. "I'm surprised to hear you talking this way."

"I don't care," Jeremy burst out. "I don't want her moving in here and wrecking all our lives!" And with that outburst he had stormed out of the room.

Dana sighed as she set Sally's picture down. Jeremy had barely been around since then, except to eat meals or to sleep. He was obviously upset, but she couldn't understand it.

Sally was family. And she was in trouble. Didn't they owe it to her to take her in and try to do their very best to give her some kind of happiness at last?

*   *   *

"Well, I guess that's everything," Sally Larson said ruefully, looking around the tiny bedroom she had been sharing with her foster sister. She couldn't pretend she was sad about leaving this house. At some of the homes she had lived in, it had been hard saying goodbye. But not this time.

She just wished she knew her cousins and her aunt and uncle a little better. It was hard enough, leaving a difficult foster family situation. But Sally knew this was the end of the road. If the Larsons didn't want her . . .

But she couldn't think that way, she reminded herself. She had to be positive. This was the day she had been looking forward to for so long—the day she had been preparing and planning for. It was finally here. She was moving in with *family*—real family!

She had to think positively. Because she knew if this move didn't work out, there was no place else for her to go.

Will Sally find a real home in Sweet Valley? Find out in Sweet Valley High #33, *Starting Over*.

SWEET VALLEY HIGH

☐	26741	**DOUBLE LOVE #1**	$2.75
☐	26621	**SECRETS #2**	$2.75
☐	26627	**PLAYING WITH FIRE #3**	$2.75
☐	27493	**POWER PLAY #4**	$2.95
☐	26742	**ALL NIGHT LONG #5**	$2.75
☐	26813	**DANGEROUS LOVE #6**	$2.75
☐	26622	**DEAR SISTER #7**	$2.75
☐	26744	**HEARTBREAKER #8**	$2.75
☐	26626	**RACING HEARTS #9**	$2.75
☐	26620	**WRONG KIND OF GIRL #10**	$2.75
☐	26824	**TOO GOOD TO BE TRUE #11**	$2.75
☐	26688	**WHEN LOVE DIES #12**	$2.75
☐	26619	**KIDNAPPED #13**	$2.75
☐	26764	**DECEPTIONS #14**	$2.75
☐	26765	**PROMISES #15**	$2.75
☐	27431	**RAGS TO RICHES #16**	$2.95
☐	26883	**LOVE LETTERS #17**	$2.75
☐	27444	**HEAD OVER HEELS #18**	$2.95
☐	26823	**SHOWDOWN #19**	$2.75
☐	26959	**CRASH LANDING! #20**	$2.75

Prices and availability subject to change without notice.

Buy them at your local bookstore or use this convenient coupon for ordering:

Bantam Books, Dept. SVH, 414 East Golf Road, Des Plaines, IL 60016

Please send me the books I have checked above. I am enclosing $_____
(please add $2.00 to cover postage and handling). Send check or money order
—no cash or C.O.D.s please.

Mr/Ms _____

Address_____

City/State _____ Zip _____

SVH—5/88

Please allow four to six weeks for delivery. This offer expires 11/88.

Get Ready for a Thrilling Time in Sweet Valley®!